ALSO BY KATHY HELIDONIOTIS

Totally Horse Mad

Kathy Helidoniotis

Horse MAD summer

HORSE MAD
2

Angus&Robertson
An imprint of HarperCollins*Publishers*

Angus&Robertson
An imprint of HarperCollins*Publishers*

First published in Australia by Banana Books in 2003
an imprint of Otford Press

This edition published in 2006
by HarperCollins*Publishers* Australia Pty Limited
ABN 36 009 913 517
www.harpercollins.com.au

HarperCollins*Publishers*
Level 13, 201 Elizabeth Street, Sydney NSW 2000, Australia
Unit D1, 63 Apollo Drive, Rosedale, Auckland 0632, New Zealand
A 53, Sector 57, Noida, UP, India
1 London Bridge Street, London SE1 9GF, United Kingdom
Bay Adelaide Centre, East Tower, 22 Adelaide Street West, 41st floor,
Toronto, Ontario, M5H 4E3
195 Broadway, New York NY 10007, USA

National Library of Australia Cataloguing-in-Publication data:

Helidoniotis, Kathy.
   Horse mad summer.
   For children aged 8–12 years.
   ISBN 978 0 7322 8421 3.
   ISBN 0 7322 8421 X.
   1. Horses – Juvenile fiction. I. Title.
   (Series: Helidoniotis, Kathy. Horse mad; bk 2).
A823.4

Cover design by Darren Holt, HarperCollins Design Studio
Cover photography by Belinda Taylor, www.bellaphotoart.com.au
Art direction and stylist: Christine Orchard
Typeset in Bembo 13/18pt by Kirby Jones
Printed and bound in Australia by McPherson's Printing Group
The papers used by HarperCollins in the manufacture of this book are a natural,
recyclable product made from wood grown in sustainable plantation forests.
The fibre source and manufacturing processes meet recognised international
environmental standards, and carry certification.

For my children,
Mariana, John and Simon,
with all my love.

ONE

Big Bucks

'Are you serious?' I stared, wide-eyed at my riding instructor, Gary Cho. He was standing on a dusty upturned milk crate, addressing the members of Shady Creek Riding Club. We were mounted on our horses, ready for inspection.

'Deadly.' Gary pushed his blue Riding Club cap up on top of his head and scratched his brow. 'But for those of us who seem to be in shock I'll say it again. The Waratah Grove Junior Cross-Country Riding Championships are coming up — open to riders from all riding clubs across the State. First prize in each age group is a thousand dollars and a four-week stay at Waratah Grove Riding Academy.'

'That's unbelievable!' I grinned at my best friend Becky Cho who smiled back, looking as dazed as everybody else.

A thousand dollars. Wow! I'd never had a thousand dollars in my life. I'd never been near a thousand dollars. I'd never even seen a thousand dollars. And for someone who'd done as much fundraising as I had to save up for a horse of my own, that was saying something. Waratah Grove was one of the best riding academies in the country. With some of the best riding instructors anywhere and top-class stables and facilities! It was booked out solidly for months and sometimes years in advance. It was the most amazing prize I'd ever heard of. A horse-crazy kid would be mad not to want to win. And it could be mine! All I had to do was be number one at the Championships.

I swallowed hard. The thought of me, eleven-year-old Ashleigh Miller from Shady Creek, getting my hands on all that money was making me drool. I toyed with my reins with one hand and patted my mare's neck absent-mindedly with the other.

'Imagine that, Honey,' I whispered, running my hand over her sleek chestnut coat. I tumbled into a delicious daydream. Honey and I were the winners at Waratah Grove and the judges were presenting us with a golden cup so huge that it would have to be semitrailered back to Shady Creek, hundred-dollar bills overflowing from it like a waterfall.

It would be tough, that was for sure, competing against the best riders in the whole State. Our chances weren't great. But it wasn't an impossible dream. And cross-country riding was just about the best fun you could have in the saddle. I'd done a bit of cross-country on Princess, my favourite horse at South Beach Stables, where I'd ridden before I'd left the city. Just not a lot.

I shook my head, plummeting back to reality. The members of Shady Creek Riding Club buzzed with excitement, dollar signs flashing like Christmas lights in their eyes.

'Try-outs will be held here at Riding Club in three weeks,' Gary said, shifting on his crate. 'So we'll be meeting here every Sunday until then. Entry is open to all members of Shady Creek Riding Club. And to make things as fair and impartial as they can possibly be, I'll have nothing to do with the judging. That will be taken care of by Amanda Filano, our local vet.'

A snort went up from Carly Barnes, Ryan Thomas and Flea Fowler — otherwise known as the Three Creepketeers — our mortal enemies. They hate Becky and me, and we hate them right back.

'There goes your chance of being on the team, Rebecca's Garden.' Carly hissed Becky's hated nickname out of Gary's earshot. 'No daddy judging means no spot for his favourite rider.'

'Like *you* have a chance,' Becky spat, her cheeks flushing with anger. Charlie, her gorgeous bay part-Arab gelding with the pure white blaze on his face tossed his head and snorted in support. 'Nobody's that desperate.'

Being called 'Rebecca's Garden' always transforms Becky from her usual calm self into an enraged maniac. It's not her fault her parents decided to name their Chinese restaurant after her. She's been begging them to change it to Trotton Inn for years.

The Creeps make out that they hate Becky because her dad is the instructor. They say she gets special treatment. But the simple fact is that Becky's the best rider in Shady Creek and Carly, Flea and Ryan hate her because they are jealous. They hate me for lots of reasons. Too many to mention. But taking Ryan's place in the gymkhana team certainly didn't help.

'Ignore them,' I said, sending Carly a look of utter loathing. Carly smirked back at me.

'How many on the team, Gary?' I said before things with the Creepketeers got out of hand.

'I was just getting to that. Unfortunately, there will be only two riders selected from the whole zone to represent each age group.'

'No way!' bawled Flea Fowler. His horse Scud, a pure black gelding, with a look in his eye as mean as his master's, pawed at the dusty ground. I can thank Scud for my hated nickname, 'Spiller Miller', which I earned after he threw me on my first day in Shady Creek. Thankfully the Creepketeers are the only ones who call me that.

Gary shrugged and pushed his hands into the pockets of his faded blue jeans.

'Afraid so. Our zone doesn't just mean us at Shady Creek Riding Club. Our zone includes Pinebark Ridge Riding Club and a few others.'

There were howls of disbelief as the Shady Creek riders saw their chances of laying their hands on that wonderful thousand-dollar prize slipping away.

'Pinedork Ridge!' Flea scoffed. 'They're all losers. All you have to do to be on one of their teams is be a total idiot.'

Not surprisingly there were loud murmurs of agreement; nobody likes to disagree with Flea. He patted Scud's hard black neck, looking pleased with himself for the trouble he'd caused.

'They can't even sit straight on rocking horses,' laughed Ryan. Ryan is almost as nasty as Flea and Carly, and follows them around doing whatever dumb stuff they tell him to. His horse Arnie is big and beefy, but has a good heart and gentle dark brown eyes. Becky and I often wonder what terrible thing he must have done in a former life to deserve Ryan in this one.

'I hear they're looking for two new members,' Carly said. 'How about it, Spiller? You and Becky are more than qualified.'

The Creeps fell apart laughing.

'That's enough,' Gary said before I had a chance to bite back at Carly. 'Pinebark Ridge is in our zone and that's the rule. And regardless of how we feel about the two-rider limit, it can't be changed.'

Everyone moaned, me included. The huge golden trophy of my dreams shrank to the size and glamour of an aluminium eggcup.

'The two riders with the fastest and cleanest runs from each age category will be representing the Shady Creek and Districts Zone at the Championships,' Gary said, hopping down from his milk crate. 'And at least one of them better be one of you!'

The members of Shady Creek Riding Club launched into a dozen excited conversations at once. I noticed Carly was sitting up straighter than usual in her saddle, smiling almost sweetly at Gary.

'Is it just me or have Carly's eyes turned into dollar bills?' I whispered. Becky snorted aloud, smothering her giggles with her gloved hand.

'Last thing!' Gary shouted over the din. 'We'll be sponsoring any member of our club who makes it to Waratah Grove. As you know only too well there's not much money in the coffers.' Gary gave his dingy office a stare as filthy as Flea's joddies. 'So we'll be doing some serious fundraising over the next month. I want brilliant moneymaking ideas from each and every one of you by the end of the day.'

I high-fived Becky and tucked my blue Riding Club shirt into my old cream jodhpurs. We moved out of our lines and trotted out towards the paddock where most of our lessons were held.

All through the lesson I couldn't stop myself from slipping back into that beautiful daydream. By the end of the lesson I was determined. No matter what happened, one of the two Under 12's representatives of Shady Creek and Districts Zone would be me.

'Can you believe it?' Becky gushed as we rode towards my house that afternoon.

'Not really,' I said, stretching my legs. After a whole day in the saddle I was pretty sore.

'I hope we both get through. Wouldn't it be amazing to go to the Championships together?' Becky beamed at me from beneath her black helmet. Her dark eyes were wide with excitement.

'You've got a great chance. Don't you remember winning Under-Twelve Champion at the gymkhana? Or coming first in dressage and jumping and winning a blue ribbon in the teams events? Charlie's the best horse around. Honey too, of course,' I added quickly so Honey's feelings weren't hurt.

'I suppose,' Becky said, pulling the blue club ribbon from the base of her long thick plait. She shoved it into her shirt pocket. 'I'm busting to get started on fundraising.'

I laughed. 'Pardon me if I'm not busting. I've been fundraising for months, remember?'

After working so hard at Horse Cents, my saving-up-for-a-horse fund, I was almost totally over fundraising. But almost everyone else at Riding Club had the fever. Becky and I had decided to clean up, decorate and sell horseshoes as lucky Christmas tree ornaments. The twins, Julie and Jodie, were planning to run a ride-in horse wash the next weekend. Carly was going to sell cupcakes (which Becky and I had vowed *never* to eat). Even Ryan was getting in on the act, offering to raffle a tank of petrol from his dad's garage. Everyone, except Flea (of course) wanted to do something.

'So, when's Jenna arriving?' Becky asked.

I beamed. Jenna Dawson is my best friend from the city. We had lived a few doors down from each other on the same street and been in the same class at the same school for as long as either of us could remember. The move to Shady Creek was a shock for both of us. But we knew that we would always be best friends. And once she and Becky got to know each other the three of us would be best friends. Best horse friends!

'Just after Christmas, in …' I scratched my chin, thinking hard. 'Twenty-eight days' time.'

I was dying for her to get here. It seemed like ages away. Thankfully there were still three weeks left of school, fundraising for Riding Club, the cross-country try-outs and our first Christmas in Shady Creek between now and Jenna's arrival to keep me busy.

'She's spending four whole entire weeks,' I continued. 'The three of us can hang out and ride and have sleepovers. It'll be the coolest fun. I can't wait!'

'I can tell,' Becky said.

We pulled up outside my place. Our horses dropped their heads and tore hungrily at the lush green grass.

'You want to come in?' I said.

Becky shook her head. 'Can't. I'm working at the restaurant tonight.'

'How about we go on a horseshoe hunt tomorrow

after school?' I pulled Honey's head up and patted her neck.

'Definitely,' Becky said. 'See ya!' She collected her reins, tapped her heels against Charlie's sides and he leapt into a neat canter.

I walked Honey down the driveway and into her corral behind the house. It's a great place, just made for horses with a stable and a barn and acres of pasture just begging to be munched on by a horse or two. I swung my legs over the saddle and slid to the ground, pulling Honey's reins over her head. She rubbed her face against my shoulder and nuzzled my pocket, looking for a carrot. I wrapped my arms around her neck and hugged her hard, feeling her warmth seep into my arms and breathing her sweet horsy smell.

'Just wait,' I murmured, untacking her. 'We're going to have the best summer. The best summer ever.'

My first summer in Shady Creek with my own horse, my gorgeous beautiful Honey: paradise.

TWO
School's In

'Hurry up, will ya, Ash?' Becky whined the next afternoon. She was tapping her watch and wriggling in the saddle. 'Charlie's dying for a run and I've been waiting for you for ages!'

I jogged around the back of the house to the corral, stuffing my school shirt inside yesterday's grotty Riding Club jodhpurs to where Honey was tied up and undid the loop of twine around her reins. She rubbed her face against my shoulder and snorted. I pulled the reins over her head, gathered them up and mounted, settling into the soft leather saddle as though it was an armchair.

'Relax, Beck,' I said, pushing my feet into the

stirrups and praying Mum wouldn't catch me riding in the top half of my school uniform. 'I was putting those horseshoes away.'

We'd done pretty well finding a boxful scattered at Riding Club, in Becky's tack shed and at Kevin's, the local farrier's place. I squeezed my legs against Honey's sides and she sprang into a walk.

'Anyway,' I continued, 'the try-outs are a whole twenty-one days away.'

'Does that include today?' Becky asked as Charlie lurched forward.

'Yep.' I wiped at the sweat that was beading on my forehead. It was late November and hot.

'Well that means the try-outs are really only twenty and a half days away.'

'I'll say it again,' I said, giggling, as we turned the horses into the grounds of Shady Creek Riding Club. 'Relax.'

'Easy for you to say,' Becky groaned. 'With the try-outs and the restaurant and school and Riding Club and scrubbing muddy old horseshoes and looking after two horses … I'm so tired!'

I felt tired just listening.

We walked our horses into the warm-up ring. Becky urged Charlie into a canter and Honey followed suit. We rode them in figure eights until they were warmed up. A little bubble of nerves tingled in my stomach. I'd never ridden Honey over cross-country obstacles before. What if she spooked at them or refused? There were only three weeks to go until the try-outs and I wanted to ride at Waratah Grove so badly I could almost taste the hot dogs.

'Quit daydreaming!' Becky yelled over her shoulder. 'Let's get started while we've got the whole place to ourselves.'

Gary had made a course of obstacles out of anything he could get his hands on. There was someone's old wooden front door, which he'd made to look like a brick wall by painting it red and drawing on black lines. There were a few logs; some on orange stands, some stacked up on top of one another and held together by thick yellow ropes. There was a jump made out of hay bales and another of old tyres threaded onto a white plastic water pipe. There were also three jumps made from fat, red and white barrels lying side by side. The course looked fantastic.

'Dad's thinking about building a coffin and digging a ditch to make a full twelve obstacles,' Becky said as we checked out the course.

'Who died?'

'Ha ha. You know as well as I do they're jumps.'

'I'm a bit nervous,' I admitted. 'I don't know much about cross-country. And I've only ever taken Honey over natural jumps, like fallen logs on trail rides and stuff like that.'

'It's pretty straightforward once you get the hang of it,' Becky said. 'And Honey's experienced.'

Honey nickered loudly and tossed her head.

'Okay, okay. I trust you,' I laughed, rubbing her mane.

'Let's walk the course,' Becky suggested, sliding down from Charlie's back.

The jumps looked larger up close, but they were solid. Gary had done a good job. Becky had been over the course a few times already.

We remounted. That nervy bubble grew larger in my stomach.

'I'll go first,' Becky said, reading my mind.

Becky lifted her saddle flap and checked her girth straps. Then she pulled her stirrups up two holes and adjusted her stirrup leathers. Once she was comfortable she urged Charlie into a trot, then a smooth canter. She circled him and rode towards the first jump, a log. Charlie cleared it easily, as though it were a twig. Next she jumped the wooden door 'brick wall'. Then the log pile and the hay bales and the tyres, another log and finally the barrels. Becky cantered Charlie back, her face flushed, her long black hair streaming out behind her like a banner. I cheered.

'That was unbelievable, Beck!'

Becky pulled Charlie up beside me.

'It was fantastic!' she gushed, breathing hard. 'I just wish there were more jumps. There can be up to twenty-five at competitions, you know.'

She slid to the ground and hugged Charlie who, with not a single hair out of place, looked like he'd just spent a week at a holiday resort instead of jumping cross-country obstacles.

'Your turn,' Becky said, loosening Charlie's girth. 'I'm going to walk him around for a bit. Cool him down.'

I faced the course. One jump, I thought. Just try one jump.

Like Becky, I checked my girth, shortened my stirrups two holes to give me some extra control, checked that my helmet was on properly and made sure my reins were buckled up in the middle.

'Get a move on, Spiller!'

The Creepketeers. My stomach went from having a nice, well-behaved bubble of nerves to having an army of angry butterflies zooming around inside it.

'Get lost, Fleabag,' I spat, gathering my reins.

'Check her out, guys,' Flea boomed at Carly and Ryan as though he'd eaten an amplifier for afternoon tea. 'Here we were thinking we'd just come down for a bit of practice and we get a free show as well. How long d'yuz reckon she'll stay in the saddle this time?'

The Creeps cackled on cue like crazed kookaburras.

The log, I thought. Focus on the log. Forget Flea and his henchmorons. Just focus on getting Honey over the jump. I willed myself to keep calm.

Honey was alert and focussed. I urged her into a trot, then an even canter. I wanted to be one with her. One mind, one body. Only then could we take the jump. We cantered in a wide circle across the paddock and turned back towards the log. Her hooves beat against the earth like a heartbeat, my heart beating along in time.

I felt relaxed and ready. The butterflies were more relaxed too. They seemed to be enjoying the ride.

'Okay, girl,' I murmured. Honey's ears flickered and I knew she understood. 'This is it.'

I pulled gently on my left rein and she moved towards the log. I could feel her long, smooth stride beneath me. The log lay ahead of us, almost daring us to jump it. It was ten metres away, then five. I pulled Honey in slightly and felt her prepare to jump. One metre now. Honey stretched out, tucking in her forelegs and pushed up with her hind legs. I felt her begin to sail over the jump and laughed out loud. Then everything went wrong. Very wrong.

It all happened so fast that even when I was lying on the ground near the jump it was hard to remember. There was a flash of yellow and a scream. I felt Honey twist suddenly in midair and myself fly from the saddle and before I could make sense of what had happened the ground smacked me hard in the guts.

All I felt after that was pain. I couldn't breathe. I couldn't speak. There was grainy dirt in my mouth. It seemed like forever until I could even open my eyes. When I did I saw Becky's face. I'd never seen her look so scared.

'You okay?' she said. 'That was bad, Ash. Just about the worst fall I've ever seen. Say something, will you?'

I sat up and grabbed my head. 'I would if you'd stop yapping at me.'

'You're bleeding.'

I felt stinging in my knees and peered at them. My joddies were torn and soaked with blood.

'Where's Honey?'

'She's over there, looking ashamed of herself.'

'My school shirt!' I groped at my uniform, panicking.

'It's fine,' Becky said, grabbing my hands and pulling me to my feet. 'Just filthy.'

'What happened?'

'You ate dirt, Spiller! Talk about living up to your name,' Flea howled, wiping tears from his eyes. 'Let's hear it for Spiller Miller! Next show's in half an hour.'

The Creeps were doubled up in laughter. Ryan looked like he'd burst his appendix. Carly had collapsed on Destiny's shoulder.

'At least Julie and Jodie will have one customer this weekend!' she shrieked.

'You idiot!' Becky screamed. 'You total, utter, complete idiot! You could have killed her.'

I rubbed my eyes and blinked at Flea. He was wearing a yellow T-shirt.

'You!' I gasped.

I could hardly believe anyone could do a thing like that. To jump out in front of a horse screaming like a banshee. I limped to Honey, my knees burning with pain. She hung her head and looked up at me.

'It's okay,' I said, stroking her firm amber neck. 'It wasn't your fault.'

I ran my hands down each of her legs, checking for injuries and kissed her face. Flea and the Creeps were still roaring. Anger welled up inside me and hot, salty tears leaked out of my eyes. I brushed them away quickly then mounted Honey and eased myself into the saddle, feeling stiff and sore. Becky was at my side.

'Good on you, Ash. Best thing to do is to get back on.'

I gathered my reins again. 'I'm not just getting back on. I'm going over that jump.'

Becky shook her head. 'You're hurt. Just go home.'

'No.'

I turned Honey away from the log and nudged her sides. She broke into a trot. My ribs ached and my knees begged me to stop but if there was one thing that fall had done, it had made me more determined than ever. I was going to beat the Creepketeers so badly at the try-outs they'd never show their faces at Shady Creek Riding Club again.

Honey stretched into a canter and for the second time I circled her wide. I looked over at the Creeps. They'd stopped laughing. They were staring at me now, with mouths hanging open like huge black caves.

I pulled Honey towards the log again.

'I trust you,' I said, feeling with all my heart that we were one again. One mind, one body. 'I trust you, Honey horse.'

We cantered towards the log. It seemed ten times the size it had been before. Honey approached it and I felt her leap, felt her soar in midair and land again smoothly as though her stride had never broken. We cantered away from the log and circled, slowing to a trot then pulled to a halt. I leant forward in the saddle and threw my arms around Honey's neck, hugging her hard. We had done it.

Becky and I rode back towards the warm-up ring to cool Honey down.

'Better close your mouth, Flea,' I said as we passed the Creeps who still looked like stunned mullets. 'You're dribbling.'

It was Becky's turn to laugh.

THREE

Lock, Stock and Barrel

'Today's the first time we'll work on our new cross-country course as a club,' Gary announced the next Sunday.

'About time,' I muttered. The clock was ticking. The try-outs were two weeks away and apart from the few jumps I'd done with Becky, I felt I was no more familiar with the rules of cross-country riding than I was with the rules of croquet. Okay, so I was exaggerating just a teeny bit. I knew some theory. But I wanted to ride. I was so itching to get onto the course I practically needed calamine lotion.

Gary squinted at the Shady Creek riders from under his cap. We were huddled around on the upturned milk crates and fallen logs that serve as an 'outdoor clubhouse'. Gary had planned the day to the last second. We'd already taken an early morning walk around the course for an up-close look at the obstacles. Theory was scheduled for before lunch when it was hot and dusty and the horses had 'sleep under a tree' much higher on their wish list than 'gallop over obstacles in the sun'. Then, finally, course work in the afternoon when the weather had cooled enough so the horses were more alert.

'So,' Gary said, looking much more relaxed than I felt. 'What do you guys know about cross-country riding?'

'Cross-country is usually part of a three-day event.' Jodie's identical twin sister Julie shot up from her crate. A dirty diamond-shaped pattern was pressed into the seat of her jodhpurs.

'Good. What else?'

'Cross-country riding as a sport originated from the role horses played in active military combat,' I said, raising my hand.

Gary pushed his cap up so high I could actually see his eyes. They were round with disbelief. 'Looks like someone's been memorising one of their many horse books.'

Flea, Carly and Ryan nudged each other and a few people giggled. I heard someone behind me say 'know-all', but I wasn't sure who it was. My face burned with humiliation. I hadn't meant to be a know-all. But I had indeed learned the whole section about cross-country riding from my book on *Horse Trials and Eventing* almost off by heart.

Gary handed around a small, stapled booklet to everyone. It was home-made, but looked very professional. The Shady Creek Riding Club emblem sat proudly on the dark-blue cardboard cover. I opened mine eagerly, as keen to learn as much as I could about cross-country riding as I was to forget about being embarrassed in front of the whole club.

Becky sat beside me on an old feed bin. She pored over the booklet, concentrating so hard she was pulling hairs out of her eyebrows.

'Has everyone managed to read all the information?' Gary asked at last.

Almost everyone nodded. By the look of him, however, Flea had fallen asleep on the grass and was using the open booklet as a sunshade.

'To summarise, there will be no less than fifteen and no more than twenty-five obstacles over no more than 4500 metres at the Championships.'

I wriggled uncomfortably on my crate. The hard plastic was digging into my bottom. It was almost impossible to concentrate on Gary's summary when my mind was mostly occupied with the sharp pains I was feeling in the seat of my pants.

'The fences will be mostly natural objects or will be natural looking. Much like those we have here. And they will tend to be blended into their surroundings. Like that barrel jump.'

Gary pointed to the barrels he'd wedged between two trees.

'That's what I mean by blend into their surroundings.'

I nodded, able to hang onto his every word now that, thanks to the crate, I had finally lost sensation from the waist down.

'The fences will be solid objects, like logs, or will be solidly made. In other words, they can't be knocked down. Water comes towards the end of the course and isn't usually too deep.'

Gary smiled at the series of open-mouthed faces

staring back at him. It was an awful lot to remember in one morning. And it was about to get worse. 'Any questions?'

'How will we be judged?' Ryan asked. I was amazed. It was the most sensible string of words to ever come out of his mouth, enough to rouse Flea from his siesta. He gawped at Ryan and scratched his head, reminding me very strongly of a baboon I'd once seen at the zoo.

'Good question,' Gary said. 'You'll be judged on a few levels. Firstly, there's time.'

He ticked a finger off on his right hand.

'There will be an optimum time, which is the best time you can complete the course in, and a time limit. You should aim to finish the course as close to the optimum time as you can before the time limit is up. If you don't you'll be given penalty points.'

'That's good, isn't it?' Jodie asked. 'I mean, shouldn't we be getting as many points as we can?'

'Not in cross-country,' I said, hoping I sounded the complete opposite of a know-all. 'The more points you have, the worse your score is. You get points for making mistakes.'

'Spot on, Ashleigh,' Gary said, smiling. 'The rider with the least points is the winner.'

'How does that work?' Jodie and Julie said in unison. 'Jinx!' They giggled at once. 'Double jinx.'

'Quit it,' Flea said.

The twins shot him a cold stare and he shut his mouth.

'Penalties are awarded if you go over the optimum time, if your horse refuses a jump or if you fall. And if the horse refuses a jump three times, you're eliminated.'

'Whoa,' I said. 'That's really tough.'

'There'll also be judges positioned at each obstacle to make sure you jump it properly and to help you if you need help.'

'How do we do that? Jump properly?' Julie asked.

Carly groaned and rolled her eyes so far back in her head that the whites showed. It was pretty creepy, but hey, that's Carly.

'For a start you have to observe the flags: red on the right, white on the left. You also have to keep the obstacle clear for the next rider.'

Gary peered at the blank faces staring back at him. I knew what he meant, but didn't dare say.

'And if you have to quit the competition for any reason, you do so at a walk and well away from the course.'

Gary grinned and rubbed his hands together. 'So, as you can see there's a whole lot more to cross-country riding at competition level than just jumping over a few logs,' he said.

There was a deep growl and he patted his stomach.

'Lunch break. Be back here in an hour.' Then he disappeared into his office.

Becky and I checked the horses and filled their water buckets before settling under a tree for lunch. As usual, she provided a Chinese feast for us to share, which we gobbled.

'My brain is hurting after all that theory,' Becky moaned, chewing on a strip of baby corn.

'Try sitting on a crate for a whole morning. Then we'll talk about pain.'

I popped a spring roll into my mouth and chewed. It tasted wonderful! I hadn't realised how hungry I was until all that food was in front of me.

'The horseshoes look great, don't they?' Becky took a long drink from her water bottle.

I nodded, my mouth too full of fried rice to say anything. They looked better than great. We had scrubbed them, scoured them and painted half of them silver, the other half gold. Then we'd glued on red and green foil angels, sprinkled on glitter and painted them again with lacquer. It had taken us all week so it was a good thing that school and homework were slowing down. All we had to do now was sell them — the perfect horse-lover's Christmas tree ornament.

I washed down my lunch with a swig of apple juice. 'All this fundraising reminds me of Jenna. She started Horse Cents off with me, you know.'

'I know,' Becky said. She handed me half a mango still in its skin, already sliced into cubes. I popped them out and sucked one into my mouth. It was so good!

'She's bound to have some great ideas. She's really smart.'

Becky wiped mango juice from her chin with the back of her hand and flicked it onto the grass. 'We already have heaps of great ideas, don't you think?'

I continued. 'Jenna's gonna love it here. Chinese food is her favourite, you know.'

'Hmm.' Becky plucked a long strand of grass and chewed on it thoughtfully.

'When she found out you had a restaurant she was so excited. She doesn't know anyone who has their own restaurant.'

Becky's face clouded over a little and she looked away.

'I just can't wait until she gets here.' I finished the mango in two more bites. 'I thought I was going to die when I had to leave her in the city. Until I met you, of course.'

Becky said nothing, but heaved herself to her feet and dusted down her jodhpurs. 'Time to head back, don't you reckon?'

We gathered our lunch things and jogged back to the corral where our gorgeous horses were waiting for us to warm them up.

My guts tumbled like a washing machine on spin cycle. My palms sweated out litres and my teeth chattered without control. I was up in three riders' time. I had already checked my girth straps at least a dozen times, but I snuck a peek under my saddle flap just in case. I probably wouldn't have been so nervous if Flea hadn't completely ruined my first attempt at cross-country on Honey. To try and distract myself, I mustered up the filthiest look I had in my power and fixed it on the Creepketeers. They were mounted on their horses, heads together, muttering away as usual. My terrible stare wasn't fazing them though. All it was doing was giving me facial cramps.

Another rider was back, which meant there were only two more riders to go until I potentially totally embarrassed myself.

'Nervous?' I whispered to Becky.

She shook her head firmly. 'No way.'

I went back to checking and re-checking my girth and examined my reins. Honey tossed her head over and over as though she was ordering me to relax. But that's the thing about orders; whenever I get ordered to do something I end up doing the exact opposite. So by the time it was my turn I wanted to be sick.

'Just once over the course and take all the time you need,' Gary said as I prepared to go.

I squinted at the first jump, trying to keep my lunch where it was supposed to be, and gathered my reins. I stared straight ahead, refusing to look back at the Creeps. Despite my fear, in a strange way I was glad I was going before Becky for once. She's my best friend, but she's a lot to live up to.

Gary clapped twice which was his signal to go and Honey leapt into a canter. I sat high in the saddle, so tense my shoulders were up near my ears. My mouth was dry. All I wanted to do was go home. So why didn't I? I had something to prove, I guess. Most of the Shady Creek riders had accepted Honey and me as part of their club. But the Creeps just wouldn't back down and there was no shortage of kids in Shady Creek who did whatever the Creeps wanted.

The first jump was the log I had fallen over. My stomach churned as we cantered towards it. I could feel Honey wanting to burst into a gallop, but I held her back, terrified at the thought of crashing to earth again. She approached the jump. I gathered my reins, moved my hands halfway up her neck and leant forward so that my seat bones left the saddle. I tried hard not to jerk on the reins, knowing I could confuse Honey into a refusal. Honey tucked her forelegs up and pushed off with her hind legs, soaring over the log. My heart thumped with relief as we touched down on the other side and cantered away clear.

I heard some faint cheers from the other riders, but as usual when I was riding, everything else was a haze of colour and sound. The only things in the whole world that really existed to me were Honey and the next obstacle. Nothing else mattered. Not wanting to beat Becky. Not even the Creepketeers.

The next few minutes were a rush of hay bales, tyres, logs, barrels and some new jumps — it happened too fast to remember them all.

The final obstacle was massive. Gary had constructed it using a tractor and with the added help of a few Riding Club parents. He had devised what looked like a log sandwich by arranging two fat logs side by side, two short ones at each end and another two on top. It was all wired together and camouflaged with small shrubs. It came up to my shoulder at least and was the only jump I was really terrified of. I had pushed it to the back of my mind using my favourite 'if you ignore it, it will go away' theory. But now it was here and Honey was galloping towards it and I had more chance of ignoring a flying horse than I did of ignoring this jump.

I readied myself, fixing my body in the jump position and felt Honey push off hard. We were suspended over the jump for what seemed like ages. I looked down from the saddle and saw the bark and wire, and leaves from the shrubs, all meshed together, all passing under us as we soared over it as one. In that moment I knew what it was like to fly, to be really free. Honey stretched out her forelegs and landed. I threw my arms around her neck crying out to her in praise. She was amazing, the best horse. Anything she wanted of me I would have given her.

We slowed to a canter and finally trotted to Gary and the Shady Creek riders. The sound of applause broke over me like waves. Gary beamed at me and patted Honey's soaking neck. I slid from the saddle and stood, shaking on the ground. It felt strange, too hard almost. I wanted that feeling back again — of flying — of being one with my Honey horse.

'Ash,' Gary said, shaking his head slowly, 'that was quite a ride, my girl.'

I couldn't speak, but nodded to show him I understood.

Becky rushed forward and wrapped her arms around my neck. 'That was awesome! That was incredible. I couldn't believe it. You were so good. Honey was so good.'

'Good,' came a voice from above. I peered up and squinted into the sun, shielding my eyes with my hand. 'But not good enough.'

Carly stepped forward on Destiny to take her turn.

For once she didn't bother me. I felt too amazing for that. But from that moment I knew one thing more than ever. I wanted to win at the try-outs. I wanted to represent the Under 12s for Shady Creek District at the Championships. I wanted to beat Carly and Flea and Ryan and Becky so badly it made me shiver.

Julie took Honey for me and led her around, cooling her down, while I unbuckled my helmet and shook out my sweat-damp hair. She gushed about our ride, but I really wasn't listening. Instead I was on a roller coaster. How could I want to beat Becky so much? The Creeps, yes. But Becky? She was my best friend. And a great rider. But I was a good rider, too. I deserved the same chances she did. It was all so confusing. Did it mean I was a terrible person? How could I love Becky to bits but want to beat the pants off her at the same time?

FOUR

The Mighty Dollar

'Dad was yapping away again last night about fundraising for the Championships,' Becky mumbled a few days later at school. We were eating lunch on the reserve between Shady Creek Primary School and the shopping centre. Bits of chewed up salad roll fell out of Becky's mouth and onto her lap. 'He reckons we're not making enough money.'

'Yuck!' I cried. 'That's totally disgusting.'

Becky swallowed and wiped her mouth with the back of her hand. 'What? Fundraising? But you're an expert, Ash. Dad's depending on you.'

'It's not the fundraising, it's your eating habits.' I giggled and leant back against a jacaranda tree. It was blooming at last. Jacarandas always remind me of Jenna and just thinking of Jenna made me grin like a loon.

Becky drank from her water bottle. 'What are you so happy about?'

'Nothing much. It's just that it's only eighteen days until J-Day. Have I mentioned that I can't wait?'

'About a hundred times an hour.' Becky packed her scraps into her lunchbox, pulled her sunhat down over her eyes and watched the lunch-time footy players intently.

'I'm going shopping with Mum tonight in town. We've got to get some stuff for Jenna's bed. And do some Chrissy shopping as well. That reminds me — I have to get a present for Jenna.'

Becky raised her eyebrows. 'Did I mention Dad and fundraising?'

'Oh, yeah.' I flushed a little. 'Sorry.'

'Julie and Jodie made a few dollars at their horse wash. And I sold two horseshoes at the restaurant last night. But he wants hundreds of dollars. Yesterday!' Becky stood up and dusted off her backside. She held out her hand and I grabbed it, pulling myself to my feet.

'It takes time,' I said, fanning my face with my free hand. 'It's so hot here. I just can't believe it.'

Becky smiled and picked up her lunch things. 'What's wrong? Didn't you have summers in the city?'

'Don't be dumb. It's just that it seems so much hotter here. More flies. More sunshine. Less air conditioning.'

We headed back towards the playground where our teacher, Mrs Hughes, had started to ring a huge hand-held bell. The Infants' kids screamed and ran around in circles, everyone else moaned. It was just too hot to be inside a classroom.

'Come over after school for a swim,' I said. 'I'm melting.'

'Better idea. Let's take the horses for a swim.' Becky's face opened into a huge, Becky-style smile. 'I'll show you how to dive off Honey.'

'Done,' I said. We shook on it and trudged to our lines, arm in arm.

'Hurry up, Ash,' Mum yelled from the back door as I cowered behind a dripping wet Honey in the corral.

'We're leaving in ten minutes. Do you hear that? TEN!'

'Keep ya hair on,' I muttered, running my sweat scraper across Honey's back. Water ran down her sides and legs in rivers. Becky and I had taken Honey and Charlie swimming in the creek. They'd had a ball, splashing and rolling in the water, but now I was late for shopping and on the verge of being in trouble again.

'What did you say?' Mum hollered.

'I said I'll be right there!' So I told a little white lie.

Mum appeared at Honey's shoulder and peered at me over her withers. 'Whatever possessed you to go horse swimming when I reminded you this morning we had a date? You look like the creature from the black lagoon.' Mum reached over and pulled a leaf from my hair.

'The creature from the creek in Shady Creek, actually,' I said, hooking my sweat scraper over the fence to dry. I grabbed an old towel from Honey's grooming crate and rubbed her down. 'It's shady by the way. Just in case you were wondering.'

Mum grimaced at me. 'I wasn't, but thanks anyway.' She stood in front of Honey and stroked her nose. 'She's so pretty, Ash. Aren't you, girl?'

I beamed. 'You know, if you ever want to have riding lessons I am the daughter to call.'

Mum shook her head. 'Not at the moment. But I promise, if I ever decide to make a fool of myself on horseback you'll be the first to know.'

I shook my head, bewildered.

'What now?' Mum said.

'I just don't know how a horsy kid like me could possibly have come from two totally non-horsy parents. It just doesn't make sense!'

'Look at the bright side,' Mum said. 'I may not be horsy like Gary Cho, but I can do something he can't.'

'What's that?'

'Install and service automatically refilling horse drinking troughs!'

She had a point.

We made it to the shops in town that night and for a few hours I managed to push the try-outs and fundraising for the Championships out of my head. It wasn't all that hard, really, what with sweating Santas on every street corner and trying to choose a Christmas present for Jenna. Finally I settled on a silver jewellery box with a delicate unicorn engraved on the lid. Perfect.

At home I curled into bed and stared at the horse calendar on the wall. I had written a single word in huge red block letters in three of the thirty-one boxes.

TRY-OUTS.
HOLIDAYS.
JENNA.

That night I dreamt of the try-outs and Honey and me riding like the wind over jump after jump and going to the Championships and winning. I held the trophy in my hands. Honey had the blue ribbon around her neck. And just this once, Becky was clapping for me.

FIVE

Winner Takes All

I had never felt so sick in my life. The try-outs were starting in ten minutes. Although it was early it was hot. My blue club shirt was already damp and stuck to my back. Becky and I were too nervous to speak. My tongue felt like a wad of cotton wool and my mouth was so dry and stiff I couldn't have managed a sentence if my very life depended on it. All we could do was nod at each other every now and then and check and re-check our tack.

I'd been over the course as many times as I could, but that didn't stop me from worrying. What if I made a mistake? What if I fell? What if we did a terrible time? And then there were the Creepketeers.

I had this feeling that they were after me again. And I knew them well enough to know they were capable of just about anything.

I had a quick look around me. Shady Creek Riding Club was the busiest I had ever seen it with three times the usual number of horses. Their riders, wearing an assortment of club colours, scurried around fixing numbers to their shirts and huddling with their instructors for last-minute pep talks. Parents dashed here and there with saddles, bridles, helmets and cold drinks. Spectators sat along the fence on folding chairs. Some were cooking sausages and onions on a huge barbecue. I could see my parents squashed together on a log, a box of our horseshoes at their feet. Horse floats were parked all the way down the road past my place. Gary had even borrowed a microphone from the local football club for the day.

'Can I have your attention, please?'

The noise stopped and everyone turned to Gary. He looked very professional with his microphone and official blue Shady Creek Riding Club uniform on, but he was standing on his old plastic milk crate, same as ever.

'I'd like to take this opportunity to welcome you all here today,' he began. I tuned out. I had to focus on the course. And on Honey.

Honey looked spectacular. I'd tried to use up a bit of nervous energy grooming her. I must have been more nervous than I thought — her chestnut coat was shining bronze in the sun. I'd even braided her mane and tail. It's true, a nice hairdo wasn't going to get us a spot at Waratah Grove, but it had helped me forget about the try-outs for a little while.

Gary wished everyone the best of luck and finished up by sending the Under 10s and 12s to their marshalling areas.

I was shaking as I led Honey to the tree that had the important job of being the Under 12s marshalling area. Rachael Cho, Becky's sister, was in charge.

'Hurry up and get yourselves over here!' she yelled through painted red lips as we straggled across. 'I haven't got all day!'

Becky rolled her eyes as we mounted our horses. 'She's got a date.'

'Really? Wow!' I whispered, adjusting my stirrups. 'Who with?'

'The mirror.'

I laughed out loud and felt much better for it. My stomach was so full of nerves I felt like a giant bottle of fizzy drink that's been shaken up, just busting to explode.

Rachael scowled at me. She thinks Becky is the biggest pain in the entire world which makes me, as her best friend, the second biggest. She opened up a folder and called off about a dozen names, including Ryan Thomas, Carly Barnes and Frederick Fowler. Everyone was there, including a few kids I recognised from the gymkhana. By the looks of it nobody under twelve in the Shady Creek and Districts Zone wanted to miss out on the thousand dollars prize money and four-week stay at Waratah Grove Riding Academy.

'You go out in the order I called your names,' Rachael said quickly. 'Wait for the bell before you start. Anyone who takes off before the bell will be penalised heavily. That's a promise,' she said, looking over her sunglasses straight at the Creepketeers who were nudging each other and rolling their eyes.

They don't like Rachael any more than they like Becky. But from what Becky has told me, they're scared stiff of Rachael. Fed up with their dumb remarks about Gary and favouritism just before she quit Riding Club, Rachael had picked Flea up by the scruff of his neck and dumped him face-first into a nice fresh cow pat. He's done his best to avoid Rachael ever since.

'Okay,' Rachael called once the Under 10s were finished. 'First up is Erica Cohen, representing Jacaranda Tops Riding Club.'

A dark-haired girl riding a cute brown New Forest pony rode to the starting line. The bell sounded and she set off.

'Carly Barnes,' Rachael called. 'You're next. Be ready to go.'

Carly kicked Destiny into a trot.

'WALK to the starting line,' Rachael barked.

'Keep yer shirt on,' Carly sneered. She just had time to turn around in her saddle, look at Becky and me and make an 'L' shape on her forehead with her finger and thumb before the bell rang. I watched them for a while. There was no denying it. Carly was good. A Creep, but good.

I was second last on the list. Becky went, as did Flea, Ryan and a kid called Joey from Pinebark

Ridge Riding Club. I hate waiting. It makes me so much more nervous. Better to get it over and done with. Honey was getting jumpy as well, so I led her round in a circle to keep her warm.

'Ashleigh Miller, you're up,' Rachael called, placing a large red tick next to my name.

My mouth went drier. I checked my girth strap for the eight-hundredth time that morning, mounted and walked Honey to the starting line, twisting around in the saddle to look for the Creeps. They were nowhere to be seen. Under normal circumstances this was cause for celebration. But today it could mean only one thing. They were planning something. I could feel it in my skin.

'You ready, dear?' said the starter.

I nodded and grunted, which she accepted as a 'yes'. Then she raised a brass bell. I gathered my reins. Honey tensed underneath me. I actually felt myself rise as her back stiffened. She danced a little on her forelegs.

The starter rang the bell and Honey burst into a gallop without even a touch from me. There was no going back now, no stopping. My heart pounded hard pushing blood through my veins faster than the legendary racehorse Phar Lap. The wind whooshed in my ears. Honey's hooves beat against the hard sun-baked ground of the course. The spectators, floats, cars and horses faded away. I should have been enjoying myself, but I was scared. There was so much at stake. And so many things that could go wrong.

'Relax,' I told myself. 'Trust your horse. She knows what to do.'

The first jump lay just ahead. I closed my eyes for a second, willing Honey to grow wings. She slowed slightly to a canter and pushed off with her hind legs and cleared it.

The brick wall was next. She soared over the obstacle. I patted her neck and told her she was the best girl. She galloped around the track to the left towards the hay bales. We cleared them, then the tyres and another log, one after the other. My heart had stopped pumping fear through my body. Now it was singing. Honey's speed and her flight over the jumps were better than anything I'd known. Better than a roller coaster. Better than laughing your guts up with your best friend in the world.

The ground rushed past under Honey's hooves. Every now and then I noticed a flash of colour or heard a burst of muffled noise from the microphone, but mostly we were alone, in our own world.

I slapped Honey's neck with my hand. 'Nearly there,' I shouted. She surged forward, jump after jump melting away underneath us. We were making incredible time. No refusals. No mistakes. No Creeps. We were going to win. I just knew it.

All that was left was the 'log sandwich'. I wasn't afraid this time. I wanted that feeling back again. I wanted to fly.

'You can do it,' I murmured. 'You can do it, Honey.'

Her hooves beat on the ground. I could smell the rising dust and noticed, for the first time, the sun warming the bare skin of my arms and the sweat soaking my palms.

I reined her in a little. The jump was a few metres away. I pulled in a little more and felt the leather slip through my sweaty hands. I panicked and grabbed at the reins, accidentally yanking hard on Honey's mouth. She tossed her head with shock, skidded to a halt and reared. I was tossed out of the saddle and up onto her neck. I screamed and clutched a handful of her mane, wrapping an arm around her neck. The jump judge rushed towards us.

'No, no!' I cried. I was so angry with myself. It was such a stupid mistake.

Honey lashed out with her forelegs and the judge backed off. I felt her falling backwards and shook my feet from the stirrups, ready to jump for my life. Just as I felt myself slipping from the saddle she calmed herself, touched down again and stood.

'You okay?' said the judge.

I nodded, shoving my feet back into the stirrups. I wiped my hands on my jodhpurs and gathered my reins, turning Honey around.

'I'm trying again!' I called.

The jump judge returned to his post.

I touched Honey's sides with my heels. She burst into a canter.

'Easy,' I murmured. 'Go easy.'

I reined her in slightly and this time she made it, taking off deep from her hind legs and soaring over the jump, landing light as a cat on the other side.

'Good girl!' I shouted. Honey gathered the last of her energy and thundered across the finish line, trying to make up for the time we'd lost. I was so proud of her. She was a champion. If it hadn't been for me we'd have made a perfect round. I hoped against all hope that the jump judge on the log sandwich would develop temporary amnesia.

Becky rushed forward as I slid to the ground. My legs were shaking.

'That was amazing!' she cried. 'You two were amazing.'

'Thanks.'

I walked Honey around for a while, cooling her down, then led her to the corral and untacked her with trembling fingers. I sponged her down and threw her blanket over her, then kissed her face. She was sticky and tired. She'd worked so hard. For that moment, being first or even last didn't seem as important as it had before because I knew my horse had run the best she could for love of me.

Finally, once the Opens had finished and Honey was fed, watered and rested, the wait was over. Becky and I clung to each other, sick with nerves. Mum hovered behind us, hopping from one foot to another.

'May I have your attention again, please?' Gary was back on the mike, ready to announce the two representatives of Shady Creek and Districts Zone for each age group. 'It is my pleasure to announce the winners of the rep spots for our zone at the Waratah

Grove Junior Cross-Country Riding Championships in a month's time.'

'Get on with it,' I thought, sneaking a look at Becky's face.

'They are Samantha McKenzie on Misty of Pinebark Ridge and Joshua Taylor on Pharaoh of Jacaranda Tops for the Under Tens.'

There was applause and cheering as the two riders rushed to the collection of upturned milk crates beside Gary that was serving as a stage.

'And for the Under Twelves,' Gary continued. 'Carly Barnes on Destiny of Shady Creek.'

Carly screamed and jumped up and down. There was a smattering of applause. She rushed to the 'stage', climbed up and hugged herself, looking as though she'd just been crowned Queen of Shady Creek.

What? I thought. How could it be? Carly? I knew she was good, but it wasn't fair. People *that* mean didn't deserve to win anything.

I glanced at Becky again. There was one place left and eleven other riders who wanted to fill it.

'And Rebecca Cho on Charlie also of Shady Creek.'

I let go of Becky and stood there, feeling numb. That jump. That mistake. My fault.

Becky screamed and hugged me then rushed over to Rachael who was standing with her friends and hugged her. Rachael did a funny dance, chanting 'Go Becky, go Becky!'

Becky took her place beside Carly and beamed.

I felt awful. Worse than awful. Mum grabbed my hand and squeezed.

'Never mind,' she said. 'Next time.'

I turned a little and looked at her, but I couldn't say anything. There were no words for the job. I'd never felt so — *disappointed* — in my life. There was a pain in my stomach, like I'd eaten a blanket for dinner and washed it down with a nice fresh barrel of wet concrete.

I didn't hear Gary announce the rest of the winners. I didn't really even hear Flea try to pick a fight with one of the jump judges, saying the whole thing was rigged. It was all just a big mess of sound. And as I watched my best friend and my worst enemy line up for the official photographs, I felt the first tears trickle down my face.

SIX

Crash and Burn

'Are you sure you're okay with this?'

I nodded at Becky and ran my hand down the back of Honey's smooth right foreleg. She lifted her foot and I stretched her leg forward, making sure none of her skin was caught under the girth.

'Don't worry about it. You deserved to win.' I stretched out Honey's other foreleg, set it down gently, gathered my reins and bounced into the saddle. Becky didn't look convinced and was toying nervously with her stirrup iron.

I'd had a whole night to get used to the idea that I wasn't going to the Waratah Grove Junior Cross-Country Riding Championships. Becky had won

55

fair and square. Carly had beaten me too, although when I thought about the self-satisfied look on her face afterwards, I wanted to throw up.

'Really, I'm fine,' I insisted, pulling my socks up and tucking my joddies into my boots. 'You're going to do great. It's a bit of a relief to tell you the truth. I'd rather paint myself in molasses and sit on a bull ant nest than stay in the same hotel as Carly for the weekend.'

'I can't argue with that,' Becky said, laughing.

'Besides, it'll give me time to do what I do best — fundraising.' I gave Honey's mane a quick scratch and patted her firm neck. 'By the way, Mum and Dad sold a dozen horseshoes yesterday!'

'As long as things are good between us, Ash. That's the main thing. If going to the Championships means losing you, I'd rather let someone else take my place. Even Fleabag.'

I leant over and stretched out my hand. 'Best friends?'

Becky clasped it and we shook firmly.

Becky and Carly had been summoned by Gary early, before it got too hot, to Shady Creek Riding Club for their first training session as a team and Becky had asked me to be there for moral support.

It seemed weird to say the word 'team' in the same sentence as 'Becky' and 'Carly', I mused, but stranger things had happened.

We put the horses through their warm-ups on the flat, starting at a trot, working in figure eights and serpentines, which are like 'S' shapes. Then moved on to a canter.

It didn't take long until Honey was moving smoothly. She, like Charlie, was hard and fit and did all that work without even raising a sweat.

We pulled up and rested in the shade, waiting for Gary. It wasn't long until the familiar white streak that was Destiny cantered down the road and into the ring.

'What are you doing here?' Carly said as she pulled Destiny to a halt, regarding me as though I was a cow pat she'd just stepped in.

'Thought I'd watch you make a fool of yourself,' I said as cheerfully as I could through clenched teeth. 'Brighten my day.'

'Touchy, touchy,' Carly sang. 'Could we be having a little attack of the jealousies?'

'Dad's here,' Becky muttered, tugging at my sleeve as I opened my mouth to reply.

I looked over my shoulder and saw Gary canter through the gates on Bonnie, his gorgeous pinto mare. Carly smirked at me, overjoyed to have had the final word.

'Morning,' Gary called, dismounting. He untacked Bonnie and filled a hay-net for her in the corral, then unbuckled his helmet, whipped it off and crammed his old blue cap on his head.

'Clear off,' Carly hissed, glaring at me.

I shook my head. 'No way.'

Gary jogged over and slapped his hand affectionately on Charlie's shoulder. 'Let's get started. Are we all warmed up?'

'Ashleigh shouldn't be here,' Carly said at once. 'Make her go home.'

Gary was used to Carly's rudeness and didn't even flinch. 'I see no reason why she can't stay. All members are allowed to use the club facilities while I'm here.'

'But you called this meeting for me and Rebecca's G— I mean Becky.'

Gary narrowed his eyes and gave her a quizzical look. He had no idea that the Creepketeers had been calling Becky 'Rebecca's Garden' for years. I smiled to myself, hoping that Carly had begun her own undoing.

'Ashleigh is a member of Shady Creek Riding Club,' he said firmly. 'She's always welcome. Now let's get started.'

Becky and I headed to the cross-country course with Carly riding Destiny close to Charlie's tail.

'Watch out!' Becky said. 'You'll clip his heels.'

Carly pulled back a little but I couldn't help thinking that clipping Charlie's heels was exactly what she had in mind.

Gary sent Becky over the course first and started his stopwatch. 'Keen to have a crack at the obstacles again, Ash?'

I nodded, squinting into the morning sun. 'Thought it would be a good idea to start early. Get the edge over the competition for next year.'

Carly stuck her finger down her throat, pretending to gag, but Gary was enthusiastic. 'That's what I like to see! You're on, Carly.'

Carly pushed Destiny past Honey and me, banging her stirrup hard against my ankle. Despite being padded by joddies, socks and leather boots, sharp pains stabbed up my leg.

'Ouch!' I snapped, glaring at her.

'Oh, sorry!' Carly drawled, her eyes gleaming with nasty delight. 'I didn't see you there.'

She kicked Destiny savagely in the ribs and the white horse leapt into a canter.

'Just hold back a second or two, Ash. Give her a chance to get a bit ahead of you.'

A second was all I waited. I urged Honey into a canter, then a gallop, pushing her so hard that within a few strides Destiny was only a couple of horse lengths ahead of us. Carly, noticing the sound of beating hooves, twisted around in the saddle and glowered.

'Just get lost, will ya?' she screamed at me, pounding Destiny's sides with her heels. Destiny stretched out, galloping as fast as she could. They moved ahead of us a few more lengths. I held Honey back, afraid to exhaust her after her effort at the try-outs the day before.

The first jump, the log, was ahead. Carly galloped madly towards it, desperate to shake me off.

'Pull her up!' I screeched. 'Slow down!'

Carly ignored me, booting Destiny hard and sending her sprawling over the log.

I shook my head, amazed she hadn't crashed right through the jump but sure that she'd won her place at the Championships with speed, not skill.

I slowed Honey as we approached the jump and squeezed her sides with my legs, gripping with my knees and moving my hands up her neck. She sailed smoothly over the jump and touched down, cantering away after Destiny.

The course straightened out as we rounded the corner and I could see Becky about five jumps ahead of us. Carly had ridden Destiny right on to Charlie's tail, a mere half a horse length behind him. I made a quick decision to skip the rest of the jumps. I was here, after all, for Becky. Honey and I had nothing to prove any more. We'd tried our best and lost. I pulled Honey clear of the course and pushed her into a gallop again.

Honey seemed a bit confused at first. She tossed her head and tugged at the reins seeming to say, 'Why are we passing the jumps? I want to jump over them!' But with the pressure of my hands on the reins urging her on and no signals from my legs to move back onto the course, she galloped straight down the track.

We were alongside Becky and Carly now who were riding the course as a race. Charlie was ahead by a nose.

'Take it easy!' I cried, ducking low to dodge a branch. They were riding so fast it would take only one spook or a clipped hoof and they could easily fall. And that speed was nothing short of deadly. They had forgotten all their training in their hunger to be first.

'Back off, Carly!' Becky yelled, riding so high on Charlie's neck she looked like a jockey.

'No!' Carly pushed Destiny harder and faster. The horse galloped on for all she was worth. Her coat had turned dark grey, soaked with sweat.

'Stop it!' I cried, swerving around a tree. 'Becky, just pull back.'

Becky ignored me or couldn't hear. They jumped and soared and galloped like they were possessed, one obstacle after the other. Becky led, then Carly, then Becky again. I rode Honey hard alongside them.

Finally the last obstacle, the log sandwich, lay ahead. I was glad not to be jumping it. Becky was a horse length ahead by now, looking over her shoulder every few seconds for Carly. Carly whipped each of Destiny's shoulders with the loop of her reins again and again. The white horse surged forward until she and Charlie were neck and neck.

'Pull him up!' I cried.

Becky reined Charlie in slightly, and leant forward. The horse stretched out his front legs and sprang from his hind legs. I could see the effort as he twisted his body over the jump. Becky rode him high and light and landed him gently. She slapped his damp neck and galloped on towards the finish.

Carly was a second behind. She dug her heels into Destiny's heaving sides and Destiny leapt forwards. It wasn't enough. The horse clipped her front hooves and panicked, lashing out at the air with her hind legs. Carly was thrown from the saddle and screamed, wrapping her arms around Destiny's neck. I was terrified the horse would fall to her knees and send Carly thudding to the hard, dusty ground, but she righted herself and cantered away, exhausted.

I was so relieved I felt weak. Carly needed a good hard fall to knock some sense into her. But Destiny didn't. Once we were back at the finish I opened my mouth to tell Carly exactly what I thought of her cross-country riding skills, but someone beat me to it.

'What was that?' Gary roared, red-faced. 'Disgraceful!'

Becky smirked at Carly behind his back and loosened Charlie's girth. Gary turned around to face his daughter.

'The pair of you!'

The smile vanished from Becky's face and she stared hard at her boots.

'What's gotten into you?' Gary raged. 'Try a stunt like that in competition and you'll be disqualified immediately if you don't kill yourselves or your horses first. I have a good mind to send two other riders in your places.'

Carly's face was red. I fought to keep the huge smile that was tugging at the corners of my mouth under control. Seeing Carly get bawled out was almost as good as Christmas.

'Cool them down. And don't either of you dare go near those jumps for the rest of the day.'

Gary turned and marched towards his office, slamming the door so hard behind him it was a miracle the whole thing didn't fall down.

I beamed at Carly. 'Keep up the good work! One more training session like that and I reckon we'll be trading places.'

'Drop dead!' she spat, turning on her heel and yanking the exhausted Destiny away.

'That was so dumb of me,' Becky said, peeling Charlie's sweat-soaked saddle blanket from his back. 'But she's been on my case for so long. I just wanted to beat her.'

I knew exactly how she felt.

SEVEN
Silent Night, Horsy Night

Honey and I had written our letters to Santa the week school broke up and I was stoked to wake up on Christmas morning to the brand-new helmet I'd been dying for and a sweet-smelling leather saddlebag with the initials A.L.M. embossed in gold on the flap. Honey was delighted with her new halter and lead rope and Mum and Dad loved the mugs I'd made for them at school.

Mum, Dad and I sat down to eat lunch on the veranda. I stared at all the food, hoping I could eat it all up with my eyes — there wasn't going to be enough room for it all in my stomach! There was cold sliced ham, chicken, huge juicy prawns, piles of assorted salads and I knew Dad would bring out his famous Christmas pudding for dessert. The only things missing were Gran, Grandad and Uncle Bill. We'd spoken to them on the phone and they'd posted us gifts, but it wasn't the same.

We yanked on crackers and each wound up with a bad joke to read out and a funny paper hat to wear.

'Let's do our toasts,' I said, watching Dad pull his pink and green hat down over his ears.

'Here's to our first Christmas in Shady Creek,' Mum said, raising her glass of apple juice.

Dad raised his. 'Here's to Ashleigh removing that blasted riding helmet at the table.'

I moaned and unbuckled it, then raised my own glass. 'Here's to Honey, and you guys, and Jenna coming in forty-eight hours and Becky whipping Carly's backside at Waratah Grove.'

Mum and Dad looked at each other and raised their eyebrows, then we clinked glasses and drank.

Later that night the three of us sat together around the TV watching a dazzling couple from Perth take out the National Ballroom Dancing Championships, our tummies bursting. Dad was still wearing his paper hat. The tree took pride of place in our lounge room, its branches decorated with metres of tinsel, an angel on top and the few horseshoes that hadn't been sold.

Sales had been good. In fact, we'd added almost eighty dollars to the Shady Creek Riding Club Waratah Grove Junior Cross-Country Riding Championships Fund, which we were happy about, but we still needed a winning idea, something to make us a lot of money and fast. It's true, I could have donated my ribbon browband money, but I needed that money to help pay for Honey's upkeep. There had to be something else we could do. I promised myself to ask Jenna what we should do the minute she arrived. If anyone would know what to do, Jenna would.

I fell asleep some time that night on the lounge with my parents at my side, my horse in her paddock and the chin-guard of my new helmet in my hand.

Thirty-six hours to go.

EIGHT

Sisters

'I can't believe you're really here!' I flopped tummy-down on my bed and propped myself up on my elbows.

Jenna Dawson scanned the cute pink suitcase lying open on her bed.

'It'll be just like old times. You and me together, all day, every day.'

Jenna looked up from her things and smiled. Her brand-new braces sparkled in the sunlight streaming through the open window. 'It is going to be great. I've really missed you, Ash.'

I sat up and hugged my knees close to my chest. 'I've missed you more!'

Jenna laughed and pulled a shimmering pink satin dressing gown out of her case.

'I can't believe your parents are letting you stay for a whole month. How are they going to survive without you? Your mum gets separation anxiety if you go and see a movie.'

Jenna shrugged and hung her dressing gown up on a wire coat hanger in her half of my walk-in wardrobe. 'Believe me, the last thing on earth my parents are thinking about right now is how much they're going to miss me.'

'Jenna, look,' I said, springing off the bed and dragging her to the window. 'We can see Honey's paddock from here. And just down there over those trees, see, is Shady Creek Riding Club.'

I pointed with one arm and slipped the other around Jenna's shoulders, squeezing her tight. It was so good to have her here with me. I was practically delirious. I wanted to show her everything and take her everywhere and transform her from Jenna Dawson Computer Head into Jenna Dawson Olympic Horse Rider all at once. I had really missed her since we'd left the city and moved to Shady Creek. It had been hard starting at Shady Creek

Primary School with the Creepketeers making sure I felt about as welcome as a botfly at a gymkhana. But this summer was going to make up for everything.

'And guess what!' I babbled, pulling her away from the window and opening the door near the end of my bed. 'Ta-da! We have a bathroom all to ourselves and Mum and Dad are lending us their old TV and video. It's going to be so cool. We'll be like sisters. I've always wanted a sister!'

'No little pain brothers barging in every five minutes.' Jenna sighed with joy and went back to her unpacking. I didn't blame her for being overjoyed. Her two little brothers are the human equivalent of tropical cyclones.

'Where are they spending the holidays?' I asked, unzipping one of the compartments in Jenna's suitcase.

She slapped my hand away. 'Grandma's.'

I hoped Jenna's poor Grandma had taken out emergency home and contents insurance.

My bedroom door opened and Mum poked her head in. She was still wearing her blue work overalls. Her hair was stuck to her face with what looked like sludge. She stank as usual, but looked happy about it.

Mum's a plumber. A perfect day for her is rolling around in a drain and sending electric eels down blocked toilets. She is not like normal mothers who scream and reach for disinfectant at the sight of disgusting slime.

'Hi, Mum.'

'Hi, Mrs Miller.'

'Jenna!' Mum said. 'It's so good to see you. Ashleigh's been driving us insane. Every day for a month now it's been "Only eighteen more days till Jenna comes ... Only seven more days till Jenna comes".'

Parents can be so embarrassing. I sent my mother desperate telepathic messages pleading with her to leave us alone and get to know a bar of soap a little better. But she continued.

'How was your trip?'

'Good. Bit long, though.'

Mum nodded. 'I bet. You two must be starved. I'll clean myself up and then we can organise some dinner.'

I wrinkled my nose and waved the air around, pleased that my skills of telepathy were having their desired effect. 'Good idea. The shower's that way.'

Mum laughed. 'Okay, okay. I know I pong. Listen, Jenna, I want you to treat our home as your own. If there's anything I or Ash's dad can do for you let us know.'

'Thanks.' Jenna smiled.

Mum closed the door. Her stink lingered.

'Tell me all the goss from home,' I begged. It seemed like years since I'd lived in the city.

'Mr Johnson is taking our class again next year, Antonio Perroto puked at the end-of-school party and Alana Ong says "hi".'

'That's it?'

'Yep.'

I had expected at least a few pleas for my return to school.

'Do you miss home?' Jenna asked, folding her underwear neatly into a drawer, which I'd emptied of horse figurines especially for her stuff.

'I missed it like crazy at first,' I admitted. 'And I especially missed you and Princess. And Holly, my riding instructor. If it hadn't been for Becky I would have stowed away on the first cattle truck out of town and come to live with you.'

'But you must be happy now you have Honey?'

'I am.' I grinned. 'I never thought I could be happy here, but Honey has made Shady Creek my home. I couldn't live without her.'

'Really?' Jenna's blue eyes were wide, as though she had never thought such a thing was possible. She just didn't get the way I felt about horses. But then, staring at a computer screen was never my thing either.

She closed her drawer and began lining up her shoes in a tidy row on the wardrobe floor. I glanced at my own pile of scuffed school shoes, black riding boots and smudged joggers all jumbled up like a muddy footwear salad.

'What about you, Jen? Looking forward to your first riding lesson? Speaking of horses, I need some of your brilliant moneymaking ideas for Horse Cents.'

Jenna chewed her bottom lip and frowned the way she always does when she's thinking. 'I don't know.'

'About riding or fundraising?'

Jenna bit down hard. 'Riding.'

'At the gymkhana you were practically busting to get in the saddle!'

'Maybe it was all the excitement. I've never really been a horse person.' Jenna frowned harder. 'Come to think of it, I've never been an animal person.'

I unhooked my old riding helmet from the back of the door and pushed it down over Jenna's fair head. 'You'll do great!'

'Maybe I should just ride a bike. Or one of those carousel horses.'

'No way,' I said firmly. I had been dreaming of a totally riding, totally horse mad summer. 'Cassata's all ready to go. She's staying here for the holidays, remember?'

'What exactly is a Cassata?'

'Rachael Cho's horse. Becky's sister. She's an Appaloosa.'

Jenna shot me a puzzled look and sat down on her bed. 'Rachael is an Appaloosa?'

'No dummy, Cassata is.'

'Why doesn't Rachael ride her?'

'Gave up riding two years ago so she wouldn't break her fingernails.' I was disgusted at Rachael. There was no way I'd ever give Honey up. Not for anyone or anything.

'And an Appaloosa is?' Jenna asked, looking totally mystified.

'A horse with a spotty brown bum.'

Jenna wrinkled her nose and frowned so hard her eyebrows crashed together. 'Sounds disgusting!'

I laughed and picked up a book on horse breeds from the floor, opening to the page on Appaloosas and passing it to Jenna. 'Cassata's a fantastic horse. You'll love her. How'd you manage to talk your parents into leasing her, anyway?'

'I didn't.' Jenna took off the helmet and tossed it back to me. 'They organised it before I even knew what was happening.'

For a moment Jenna sounded so sad. Thinking she was just homesick I sat next to her and nudged her gently in the ribs.

'We're going to have the best time. You'll love it here. You'll love Riding Club. And you'll love Becky!'

Jenna gave me a small smile and went back to her unpacking.

'Staying a whole month with Ashleigh Miller the slob of the south is going to be a bigger challenge than staying on a horse!' she moaned.

I threw my pillow at her and laughed. This holiday was going to be unreal.

NINE

Moments of Truth

I hadn't felt so sick since getting stuck on an out of control teacup ride at the Shady Creek Primary School Spring Fete. My two best friends were meeting each other for the first time and I wanted it to be perfect.

I hooked my arm through Jenna's as we stood in the driveway, watching Becky ride Cassata towards us.

'She's going to love you,' I whispered. I hoped!

Becky pulled Cassata up at my feet and slipped down from the saddle. She unbuckled her helmet and smiled, handing me Cassata's reins.

I took a deep breath, like someone getting ready to make the most important speech of his or her entire life. In a way, it was. 'Becky Cho, meet Jenna Dawson. Jenna, this is Becky and Cassata.'

Jenna nodded her head and smiled nervously. 'Hi.'

I waited for the magic to start.

'Hi,' Becky said.

Okay, maybe magic was a bit unrealistic, but fireworks weren't too much to hope for, surely. A sparkler would have done at the very least.

'So this is Cassata.'

'Yeah,' Becky said.

'Can I call her Cassie?' Jenna stroked the tip of Cassata's nose.

'What a cute name for her!' I cried. 'How come I never thought of that?'

Becky frowned. 'Her name's Cassata. But I s'pose it'll be all right.'

Jenna looked at her feet for a while. Becky looked at the sky. I chewed on my bottom lip.

'Why don't I put Cassata's tack away while Jenna gets to know her a bit?' Becky said at last.

I was ready to collapse with relief. My legs were feeling like two towers of wobbly jelly.

Becky and I untacked Cassata and I led her into Honey's paddock, Jenna at my side. Becky disappeared into the tack shed with Cassata's saddle.

I showed Jenna how to close the gate and tied Cassata to a tree.

'Let's give her a groom. It'll help you get to know her. And she can check you out as well.'

I showed Jenna how to use the old body brush, running it over Cassata's dark-brown, black and white spotted rump again and again. Her muscles rippled with pleasure and her head drooped. In no time she was almost asleep.

'It's like a massage, eh girl,' I said. 'Maybe even better.'

I handed Jenna a rubber currycomb.

'That's for the mud on her legs and belly. Don't be too rough though.'

Jenna scratched at the mud that had dried on Cassata's belly while I picked a few leaves from her tail.

'Listen,' she said after a while. 'I just wanted to say sorry.'

I ran my hand down Cassata's right foreleg, pushing gently against her shoulder until she lifted her foot and then I pulled a silver hoof pick out of the back pocket of my jeans. 'For what?'

Jenna threw the currycomb into the box I kept all the grooming gear in and sighed.

'I've been keeping something from you for a long time.'

I placed Cassata's clean hoof on the ground and straightened up immediately. The hoof pick hung from my fingers, practically forgotten. What could she have been hiding from me? My mouth dried out. I choked out the word. 'What?'

'I should have told you ages ago.' Jenna stroked Cassata's forehead. 'I've been busting to tell you, but I wanted to see you first. Face to face.'

My stomach churned with a terrible feeling. Did Jenna have a new best friend?

I unbuckled Cassata's halter, slipping it off over her ears. The groom was finished for now. She trotted over to Honey. The two horses greeted each other nose to nose and got on with the serious business of grazing.

'Well, it's just that you don't know what's going on. I should have told you before, but I couldn't.'

'Told me what?' I was starting to feel desperate. 'What is going on?'

I realised for the first time how tired Jenna looked. She seemed older and sadder, like she'd lost her sparkle.

Jenna slumped against the tree and slid to the ground. 'It's Mum and Dad. They split up.'

'You're joking!' I gasped.

'Don't be dumb,' Jenna moaned. 'Do I look like I'm joking?'

'No. Definitely not.'

Jenna's eyes filled with tears, she rubbed at them with the backs of her hands but it wasn't enough to stem the flow. She pulled a wad of tissues from her shirt pocket.

'Are you sure?' I asked, hoping she was making a mistake. I'd known heaps of kids at school, here in Shady Creek and in the city, whose parents had split up, but it wasn't supposed to happen to Jenna.

Jenna sniffled loudly and wiped her nose with a crumpled pink tissue. 'Believe me, I'm sure. That's why I was sent here. To get me out of the way while they sell the house. By the time I get back they'll be in new places.'

'But why? What happened?'

Jenna shrugged, no longer bothering to brush away the tears rolling down her face one after the other. 'Who knows? I mean, they fight. But everyone does, right?'

She gave me a look like she wanted me to say it was all a lie. That she was having a bad dream she could wake up from.

'Mum said something about adult relationships being complicated but I think that's garbage. If they wanted to they could work it out.'

I didn't know what to say so I slipped my arm around her shoulder. She was shaking and started to cry really hard.

'I just can't believe it! I'm so scared.'

'It'll be all right, Jen,' I whispered, squeezing her.

'Who are we going to live with? What if they make me choose? What if they marry other people? What if they have more kids and forget all about us?'

'One disaster at a time,' I said.

If it was possible, she cried even harder.

We sat together until Jenna was finished. She leant into me, exhausted but looking like she felt a little better and gave me a weak smile.

'Ashleigh, I'm just so glad I came here. I'm so glad I still have you.'

I leant my head against hers. Our shoulders pressed together.

'You'll always have me, Jenna. No matter what.'

'But you have to promise me something.'

'Anything,' I said.

Jenna looked straight into my eyes and hooked her pinky finger around mine. 'You can't tell anyone about this.'

I glanced over at Becky who was sliding the bolt across the door of the tack shed.

'Not even Becky?'

Jenna's blue eyes widened and she shook her head. 'No. Now promise me.'

I bit at my bottom lip as Becky slipped through the fence and jogged across the paddock to our tree. 'I promise.'

We shook pinkies on it.

The only sound in the dark, still bedroom late that night was Jenna's slow breathing. I smiled to myself. It was weird, but nice all at once. Unfortunately it was also distracting. I'd been lying there for what felt like hours and hadn't been able to sleep. But my head had been so full of thoughts. The try-outs, the Championships, Jenna, Becky, the Dawsons, my mum and dad, Honey, Cassata ... They all swirled around and around my mind like a kaleidoscope. It didn't help things at all that it was hot and sticky and opening the windows would only invite an army of mozzies in to have their dessert on my legs.

I tossed back the sheets and slipped out of bed, padding barefoot across the floor and out into the hall. Jenna slept on, oblivious. She had seemed happier since she'd told me about the divorce, like some terrible burden had been lifted from her shoulders.

I headed down the hallway, past Mum and Dad's room. The door was ajar and I could see Mum sleeping diagonally across the bed. The light was on in the kitchen downstairs so I set off towards it like a little moth.

Dad was inside eating dinner at the table. I had a look at the clock high on the wall above the window. It was nearly midnight.

I coughed. Dad looked up, surprised.

'You scared the life out of me, Ash.'

'Sorry,' I said, sliding into a chair.

Dad looped some spaghetti onto his fork. 'What are you still doing up?'

'Couldn't sleep.'

He smiled. 'Jenna snoring?'

'Nothing like that.'

'That's good,' said Dad. 'Your mother's snoring keeps me awake sometimes.'

He chewed his forkful of spaghetti and swallowed, frowning. 'How's Mum been tonight, by the way?'

'Fine,' I said, thinking the red stains on his white uniform indicated he really should be wearing a bib. 'Why?'

'She was feeling a little off-colour this morning.'

I watched him eat for a while.

'Dad?'

'Humph.'

'If there was something wrong you'd tell me, wouldn't you?' I studied his face intently.

He put down his fork and took a long drink of water from a glass. 'You know we always try to be honest with you, Ashleigh.'

I folded my arms. 'You didn't tell me about the move to Shady Creek.'

'Well, um. No.'

'Or about us having money problems before Mum found a job.'

'Okay, okay. I give up.' He held his hands up in mock surrender. 'You win, kiddo.'

Dad pushed his seat back, got up and went to the fridge. 'How about a nice hot chocolate? Help you sleep.'

'Dad, it's boiling.'

He yawned and scratched his beard. 'Too true. Sometimes I really miss that air conditioner we had back home. Bedtime story?'

I rolled my eyes. 'I'm eleven.'

Dad smiled wistfully. 'So you are. Although I do not believe you can ever be too grown-up for a bedtime story.' He reached over and tousled my hair. 'Glass of water, then?'

I nodded. 'Thanks.'

'So, what's bugging you?' he asked.

'Flea.'

'Ha, ha.' He opened the fridge and rummaged for the water jug. 'I just saw it not two minutes ago. Ah. Here it is behind the tomato relish. What is it really?'

'Did you know about Jenna's parents?'

I'd pinky promised, I know. But I had to find out.

'Yes,' he admitted. 'But we didn't think it was a good idea to tell you.'

Dad poured water into my favourite yellow horseshoe-print mug.

'Why not?'

'That was up to Jenna. Not us. It's her business. Besides, we knew she'd tell you when she was ready.'

'I s'pose.'

Dad set the water down in front of me and went back to his dinner. I took a long drink and slumped in my chair.

'Dad?'

'Yep?'

'If there was something going on between you and Mum, something bad, would you tell me?'

Dad smiled at me. 'You'd be the first to know.'

I grinned, relieved, but overcome by sudden exhaustion. My eyes felt like balls of solid lead.

'Now drink up and get to bed.'

Who was I to argue with that?

TEN

Hot Seat

'Go on, Jenna. Mount.'

Jenna spun around in the centre of the corral at Shady Creek Riding Club. 'What mountain?'

She was decked out in a pair of brand-new black riding boots, my old beige jodhpurs and my old helmet. It was her first-ever riding lesson and she looked great.

I patted the seat of Cassata's saddle. 'Mount Cassata. Get up on her back.'

'How?'

I looked up at Becky, already feeling a bit helpless. Riding came so naturally to me I couldn't understand how anyone could know nothing about it. I just had to get Jenna in the saddle. Gary was on his way to collect her for her lesson. Honey was tacked up and tied to the fence, waiting for me.

'It's easy,' I said. Jenna chewed on her bottom lip, looking pale. 'Just grab hold of the pommel at the front of the saddle with one hand and the back of the saddle with the other, stick your left foot in the stirrup and bounce up. Then swing your right foot over the saddle and sit down. Easy.'

'Right.'

Jenna sized Cassata up for a moment. The Appaloosa blew sweet warm breath over Jenna's face as if to say, 'you'll be okay'. I held on to her reins although there was really no need. Cassata is one of the gentlest horses I've met. A push-button pony. She was the perfect horse for Jenna to learn on.

Jenna swallowed and pulled at the chin-guard of her helmet. 'This thing is choking me.'

'Come on, Jen.' I patted the saddle again. Becky, thinking I wasn't looking, glanced at her watch. She was waiting for me. We'd planned to leave Jenna with Gary and jump the cross-country course together, but now I wasn't so sure. It looked like Jenna really needed me.

'Here goes.'

Jenna grabbed the stirrup and slid her left foot in. She held onto the saddle so tight her knuckles were white. With a few bounces she was sitting in the saddle.

I clapped and handed Jenna the reins. She took them with one hand, the other clinging to the pommel.

'See,' I said, relieved. 'You made it, Jen. It's all downhill from here.'

Somehow that hadn't come out like I'd planned.

Jenna frowned. 'That doesn't sound so good. Don't say anything with the word "down" in it while I'm sitting up so high.'

'You look great up there.' Gary opened the gate of the corral and smiled at Jenna. As usual, his old blue Shady Creek Riding Club cap was pulled down low over his eyes.

'She's all ready for you,' I said.

'Just move your leg back a bit for me, will you, Jenna?' Gary lifted the saddle flap and checked the girth straps. 'Needs at least two more holes, Ash. She's filled herself with air.'

I blushed, annoyed at myself, wanting everything to be perfect for Jenna.

Gary held Cassata's reins under her chin and led her towards the warm-up ring. 'By the end of the hour we'll have a champion on our hands. Right, Jenna?'

She gave me a pitiful look and waved farewell as though she was being taken off to her execution.

I watched Jenna being led into the ring. Gary had her dismount and began pointing to different parts of Cassata and the saddle, naming them. Jenna squinted with concentration.

'Let's get going,' Becky said urgently.

I frowned, not really knowing what to do. 'Maybe you should go without me.'

'What do you mean? We always train together. You and me against Carly equals a fair go, right?' Becky gathered her reins.

I was in agony. Becky needed me; Jenna needed me. For the first time ever I had to choose between my two best friends. It was awful.

I scuffed at the hard earth with the toe of my boot and looked up at Becky. 'I really should stay with Jenna. It's her first time.'

I wanted to tell Becky about Jenna's parents and how upset she was. I'd heard Jenna crying when her mum had called and she'd barely eaten anything since she arrived. Jenna needed me now more than ever.

'Okay,' Becky said. She nudged Charlie's sides with her heels. 'I'll see you later then.'

I turned my attention back to Jenna who was leading Cassata around. Jenna looked happier to have her feet back on the ground and was actually managing a smile. She saw me watching her and waved and I knew I'd made the right choice.

'Jenna, it can't be that bad.'

Jenna was lying face down on her bed with an icepack over the seat of her jodhpurs, whimpering like a lost puppy.

'At least let me look,' I said, trying to prise the icepack away with my fingers. 'You may have saddle sores.'

'There's no way you're looking at my bum!' Jenna clamped both hands over the pack. 'I don't care how long we've known each other.'

'Do you want me to call Dad? He is a nurse, after all.'

Jenna looked horrified at the thought. 'Get serious!'

Becky hovered in the doorway of my bedroom saying nothing, a funny smile on her face. I couldn't tell what she was thinking.

'What's wrong? You've been like this since we got home from Riding Club.'

'I'll never walk again!' Jenna wailed. 'I'm in agony. My butt is broken, and my legs and everything else.'

'You're going to be a teensy bit sore until you develop your seat, Jen. It's all part of learning to ride.'

'Funny how you never mentioned that this morning,' she sniffed, turning her blotchy red face up to mine. 'And besides, what have seats got to do with it? I won't be able to sit on a seat for the rest of my life. How can you be so insensitive?'

'I think you could be exaggerating,' I said, sighing slightly.

'I've never been in so much pain, ever,' Jenna cried, twisting around a bit and poking her backside gingerly with the tip of her index finger. 'OW!'

I grinned at Becky, rolling my eyes a little. She gave me a small smile but backed away until she was standing in the hall alone.

Then I had an idea.

'How about a swim, Jenna? You've just got a slight case of rider's bum. It'll do you good.'

Jenna's moaning stopped instantly. She sat up and placed her icepack on the bedside table. 'A swim? In your pool?'

'Down the creek.'

'*Cold* water?'

I nodded.

Jenna leapt off the bed and to her drawers, rummaging neatly. She pulled out her brand-new blue swimmers, snapped them against my legs and made it to the bathroom in two steps.

'Ready when you are,' she sang, slamming the door. 'Mind you my butt will probably sizzle as I hit the water. It really is killing me. It's actually *hot*!'

'Great,' I said, clapping my hands. 'Becky and I'll go get the horses tacked up.'

Jenna wrenched the bathroom door open, one hand clamped over her bum protectively. 'Horse riding?'

I nodded again.

'Don't tell me we're *riding* to the creek.'

More nodding.

'But why? Haven't I had enough for one day?'

'You've only had one lesson,' I said. I glanced at Becky who was looking hurt. She loves Cassata and riding as much as I do and she seemed to be taking Jenna's rider's bum very personally. I realised then I'd forgotten to fill Becky in on the Jenna-and-horses details. That's because there weren't any. She'd always been kind of scared of horses. 'Let's just ride to the creek. It's not far. We'll swim the horses. It'll be fun.'

Jenna nodded slowly. 'Okay.'

I sighed, relieved. 'Great.'

Jenna disappeared back into the bathroom to change. Becky and I jogged downstairs to catch the horses. We collected our bridles from the corral.

'We can ride bareback,' Becky said as we squeezed through the fence and into the paddock where the horses were grazing.

'I'll double Jenna,' I said.

Becky nodded tightly and called Charlie. He looked up and whinnied at the sound of her voice.

'Are you okay?' I asked Becky, searching her face.

I hadn't seen her like this since the very first day we met, when the Creeps were giving her a hard time.

'Yep,' she said, avoiding my eyes.

'Tell me,' I said, grabbing her arm and swinging her around to face me.

'I just did,' Becky mumbled. She looked into my eyes for a moment. 'Are we going for a swim?'

Charlie walked to her and rubbed his face against her shoulder. She undid his halter and looped it over her arm, slipping the silver bit into his mouth.

I called out to Honey. She looked up briefly, then went on grazing, leaving me no choice but to go after her.

'Greedy guts,' I said as I approached her. She snorted and shook her head. I ran my hand under her neck and slipped the bridle over her nose. I led her back to the fence where Jenna and Becky were waiting.

In less than twenty minutes the three of us, Honey and Charlie were up to our necks in the cool clear water of the creek. Becky entertained us with a series of amazing horse gymnastics.

'That was awesome, Beck!' I yelled as she surfaced after doing a perfect back flip into the water from Charlie's rump. The bay gelding gazed at his mistress and snorted water out of his nose.

Becky paddled back to Charlie and slipped onto his back, which was only just above water level. Her waist-long black hair shone like wet silk.

'Now you try, Jen.' I slapped Honey's wet rump.

Jenna swallowed and chewed her bottom lip, but scrambled onto Honey's back, dangled a leg from either side and inched down to her rump. She stood, shaking, and looked at me for a moment, terror etched on her face. I gave her the thumbs up.

Jenna balanced on the edge of Honey's wet, golden syrup-coloured rump. Just as she was about to dive, Honey tossed her head. Jenna twisted around and lost her balance.

Right then I knew that no matter what, she couldn't save herself. I wanted to cover my eyes. It was like coming to the worst part of a scary movie. You want to close your eyes, to let it all happen without you, but you just can't. So I watched as Jenna did the world's biggest ever belly flop into the creek. SMACK! I could almost feel the pain. Then she disappeared under the water.

'Jenna!' I screamed. I didn't know what to do. I dropped Honey's reins and charged towards the blue and blonde stain that still hadn't broken the surface. The water felt like wet concrete all around me, dragging at my arms and legs and refusing to let them work properly.

Just as I got close to Jenna she surfaced, spluttering. Her hair was plastered to her face like clumps of limp spaghetti.

'Jenna!' I said, hugging her hard. 'That was some dive!'

I let her go and beamed. She wheezed a little, scraping the water out of her eyes, getting her breath back after a few loud gulps.

'You have to believe me,' she panted. 'Computers are much less of a health hazard. I just don't understand how you can be so nuts about horses!'

'And I just don't understand how you just don't understand!'

'I'm really trying, Ash. For you,' Jenna said.

We hugged again, laughing. And that's when I noticed Becky.

She had ridden Charlie out of the creek and was sitting on his bare back on the bank, dripping wet, watching Jenna and me with sad, dark eyes. I realised right at that moment I had looked the same way on my first day at Shady Creek Primary School, the day Becky had rescued me from the Creepketeers and we'd become best friends.

'Becky, what are you doing?' I called.

'Gotta go,' she said. 'Charlie needs a rest before tomorrow morning.'

'What's going on tomorrow morning?'

'Training. Don't you remember? You said you'd be there.'

'Oh.' I pushed my dripping hair out of my eyes and waded out of the creek. Jenna held Honey's reins nervously.

'About tomorrow,' I said once Jenna was out of earshot. 'I thought I'd take Jenna into town. Show her around.'

'But you said you were coming to training.' Becky's face was pinched. I felt horrible.

'I know. But Jenna's only staying for a month. I really wanted to spend some time with her.'

'Can't you do that at Riding Club?'

I stroked Charlie's forehead and sighed. 'Horses aren't really Jenna's thing. They never have been. Look!'

Jenna was gesturing frantically for me to hurry up and save her from Honey. Honey was standing in the water as placidly as a rocking horse.

'Besides, we'll be there in the afternoon for her lesson.'

'Suit yourself,' Becky said. She nudged Charlie with her bare heels. 'I've gotta go.'

With that, she turned and disappeared down the track.

I trudged back towards Jenna feeling like the worst kind of traitor. I knew that Becky needed me to be at Riding Club to join forces with her against the Creeps, but Jenna needed me too.

Jenna threw me Honey's reins and splashed a handful of water into my face. 'Remember all those water fights we used to have at the pool?'

I splashed her back, laughing like a maniac. It felt like old times. Maybe this holiday could still be perfect.

ELEVEN
Back in the Saddle

'Jenna, you've got to relax!' I yelled the next afternoon. 'Don't stick your chest out so far.'

Jenna hunched her shoulders forward, clinging to Cassata as the Appaloosa ambled around the warm-up ring at Shady Creek Riding Club. Becky and I watched her every move like a pair of Olympic judges. Becky had been pretty quiet since I'd arrived at Riding Club with Jenna. When I'd asked her how the morning training session had gone she'd shrugged and said 'okay' and nothing else.

'Now you're slouching,' I added. 'Sit up a bit. You look like a question mark!'

Jenna obeyed, though she looked as if she'd just

been told the school holidays were cancelled. But I was determined. Jenna was going to be a hot rider by the end of the summer holidays whether she liked it or not. I fired tips at her like an out of control tennis ball machine.

'Smile. Pretend you're at dance class.'

'Let go of the pommel; you won't fall.'

Jenna swallowed hard. 'Stop the horse,' she wailed. 'I want to get off!'

'Keep your socks on,' I laughed. 'And point your heels down.'

'Not that far down,' Becky cried, clutching her forehead with both hands. I looked at her, surprised. It was the first thing she'd said to Jenna all afternoon.

'Your hands are up way too high. Hold them just above Cassata's withers.' I squeezed Becky's hand. She turned to me, her dark eyes solemn.

'Her *what*?' cried Jenna.

'Her withers,' I said. 'You know, that lumpy thing at the base of her neck.'

'Oh, that.'

'Good,' I said. 'Now try reining her in.'

Jenna pulled hard on Cassata's reins. I flinched. The horse tossed her head and stopped suddenly.

'Don't!' Becky said, sprinting to Cassata. She grabbed her reins, inspecting the corners of her mouth. 'You could have really hurt her.'

'I'd never hurt Cassie.' Jenna looked upset. Her eyes filled with tears.

I was trying to be gentle with Jenna, to ease her into riding and try to help her forget, even a little bit, about her parents. I knew how horrible things were for her. But Becky didn't know a thing. It made me feel like the ham in the sandwich.

Jenna shook her feet from the stirrups and slid to the ground as though she was sliding down a cliff face.

'I think I've had enough for today.' Jenna hobbled past me and out of the ring, leaving Becky gawking after her, Cassata's reins still in Becky's hands.

I watched Jenna limp out of the gate, feeling thoroughly miserable, not knowing what to do.

'What's with her?' Becky said. 'What did I say?'

'Things aren't great for her right now.' I took Cassata's reins from Becky.

'What's that supposed to mean? What's going on?'

I bit my bottom lip, knowing I'd said too much already. 'I'm not supposed to say.'

Becky grabbed my arm. 'That's not fair! If you know what's bothering her you should tell me.'

My insides wriggled like a barrel of worms. 'I can't, Becky. I promised Jenna. It's a secret.'

Becky's eyes flashed. 'We don't have any secrets. We always tell each other everything. That's what best friends do.'

I looked at the ground. She was right. We were best friends. There had never been any secrets between us. But I was Jenna's best friend, too.

I shook my head. 'I can't tell, Beck. I just can't.'

Becky's mouth dropped open. We'd never argued before. Just as she was about to speak we heard a horribly familiar sound.

'Your friend's a hot rider, Spiller. It's easy to see who's been teaching her. She's got that style about her. That certain *Spiller* style.'

'Why don't you just go and play in the traffic, Fleabag,' I screamed, all the stress of the last few days bursting out of me like an erupting volcano. I'd had it completely with the Creepketeers.

'I would, but there's no traffic in Shady Creek,' Flea said coolly. He squinted at me like an alien trying to decide which horrible experiment to do on me first. So did Scud.

'Why don't you go find some and try it out for me?'

Carly glared down at us from Destiny's back. Her eyes were mean and cold. Her red hair was bound in its usual tight bun at the base of her skinny neck. 'It's our turn now so you losers can clear off.'

'Your turn for what?' Becky said, stepping forward. Even though I was upset about our argument I couldn't help thinking how brave she was.

'None of your business,' Carly snapped, her ears going a little pink.

'It's totally my business. Dad says nobody's allowed to use the rings when he's not here without telling him first. You know that's the rule.'

'Well, of course I know that's the rule,' Carly mimicked, shaking her finger. 'But I never said we were using the rings. We're using the cross-country course.'

'C'mon, Becky,' I said, tugging at her sleeve. I wanted to leave before there was trouble. But more than anything else I just wanted to get home to Jenna. 'Let's get out of here.'

'You're right,' Becky agreed. 'They need all the practice they can get.'

I led Cassata towards the gate of the warm-up ring with Becky at my side. Carly slid out of the saddle and stood in front of us, blocking our way. She folded her arms and glowered at Becky.

'You may have won dressage at the gymkhana,' she began. I actually felt a bit sorry for her. It must have been awful to say it out loud. She looked like she was trying to lay an egg.

'And the jumping.' I couldn't resist.

'Butt out,' Carly barked, turning on me.

'And Under-Twelve Champion,' I said, thoroughly enjoying myself.

Carly stepped up close to me and pushed her face into mine. She was so close I could see myself reflected in her eyes and smell the raspberry jam sandwich she'd had for lunch. Her ears had gone from pale piggy pink to deep red.

'I'm warning you.'

My heart jumped. Carly had a habit of being really scary. People whose eyes are that cold usually are.

She turned on Becky again, narrowing her eyes. 'Forget about representing Shady Creek and Districts at the Championships, Rebecca's Garden. I'm going to make you wish you'd never even looked at a saddle much less sat in one.'

She turned her cold eyes back to me. 'Your little friend better not even *think* about turning up at Riding Club. Not if she knows what's good for her.'

With that, Carly sprang onto Destiny's back and the Creeps cantered away towards the cross-country obstacles.

'You going to tell your dad they're using the course?'

'No choice,' Becky said miserably as we walked Cassata back to my place. 'He has to know. Just gives them another reason to hate me.'

'Don't worry.' I slipped an arm around her shoulder. 'It's all part of the fun of living in Shady Creek.'

Becky laughed and patted Cassata's neck. My thoughts turned to Jenna.

'Please be patient with Jenna. If you give her time, she'll tell you what's going on.'

'It's still not fair. I tell you everything.'

I sighed. 'Becky, please don't be upset with me.'

She frowned, refusing to look at me. 'I'm not. It's just that ...'

'What?'

'It's like I only just find you and she ... never mind.' Becky's face flushed and she broke into a trot.

'Becky, wait!' I called. But by then she was running. I called her name again and again but she kept on running until she disappeared around the corner. I stopped and buried my face in Cassata's neck, feeling the first tears sting my eyes. In that instant my dreams of a totally horse mad, perfect holiday with my two best friends melted away like ice cream on a summer day.

TWELVE
Toeing the Line

The next day Becky didn't show for the lesson we'd planned for Jenna in our paddock. I tried to convince myself that she was busy preparing for Waratah Grove, but in my heart I knew the truth. I'd hurt Becky without meaning to, without even knowing I'd been doing it. I tried to push my feelings aside and concentrate on Jenna, but it wasn't easy.

Jenna was mounted and ready to go. I hadn't told Jenna about Becky. Jenna had enough to worry about. But it was getting hard, keeping all those secrets locked inside.

'Isn't Becky coming?' she asked.

'I … ah … She's not feeling well. She called before,' I stammered out my little white lie.

'When?' Jenna peered down at me from Cassata's back.

I scratched at my fringe, thinking hard. 'Before. Ready to get started?'

Jenna nodded. 'As I'll ever be.'

'This,' I said, holding up a long red rope, 'is a lunge line.'

Jenna frowned and raised an eyebrow. 'What does it have to do with me?'

'I'm going to clip it to Cassata's cavesson — the special headstall that she's wearing under her bridle,' I added, noticing the mystified expression that had swept across Jenna's face.

Jenna patted Cassata's neck while I secured the lunge line. 'Lunging is a great way to develop your seat. You can also get a bit of practice trotting without worrying that she'll get out of control. Ready, Freddy?' I grinned. Jenna nodded slowly and grabbed at the reins.

I stepped forward. 'Uh-uh. No reins.'

'What? How can I ride without reins? It'd be like driving a car without a steering wheel.'

That familiar look of terror crept back into Jenna's eyes.

'You have a steering wheel,' I said, shaking the lunge line at her. 'Me!'

Jenna leant over to check that her feet were firmly wedged in the stirrups.

'Uh-uh,' I said again, shaking my finger like a cranky teacher. 'No stirrups either.'

'I'm getting off,' Jenna said automatically. She was on the ground before you could say 'palomino'.

I gave her a look and handed her the lunge line, unclipping it from Cassata's cavesson.

'I'll show you what to do.' I pulled on Jenna's helmet and mounted Cassata. Once I was comfortable in the saddle I removed the stirrups and tossed them into a clump of grass near the fence.

'First thing is to do some stretches in the saddle. Like this.'

I demonstrated a few easy toe-touches and some arm swinging. Jenna watched with huge blue eyes.

'Now for the good stuff. Walk on!'

Cassata, responding to my voice and the signals from my legs, began a slow circular amble. I didn't have to work very hard to stay in the saddle. She was so perfect for Jenna, such an easy-going horse. I couldn't figure out why Jenna was so scared.

'Trrr-rot!' I called. Cassata jerked awake and began to trot slowly. 'Watch this, Jen. Horizontal arms.'

I stuck my arms straight out, like wings, and settled into a good natural rhythm with Cassata's strides. 'Lunging is a great way to correct any mistakes you're making in the saddle. Once you've found the right position, the rest just happens. Like magic. Cannn-terrr!'

Jenna watched as Cassata cantered around the paddock with me stirrup-less and rein-less on her back. Finally I called to her to halt. I beamed at Jenna, my problems with Becky temporarily forgotten. That's the way it always was. My worries melted away once I was in the saddle.

'Now it's your turn.'

I threw my leg over the saddle and slid to the ground, unbuckling the helmet.

Jenna put it on again and I gave her a leg-up. She crouched low in the saddle; hanging onto the pommel so hard her knuckles were practically transparent.

I clipped on the lunge line again and let it out, walking to the centre of the paddock.

'Are you sure about this?' Jenna called.

'It's easy,' I said. 'Ready to go?'

Jenna was pale under her helmet but she nodded.

'Walk on!' I called.

Cassata moved into a nice easy walk. Jenna was bent almost double, hanging onto as much as she could.

'Sit up!' I cried. 'Let go of the pommel.'

Reluctantly, Jenna did as she was told.

'Now put your hands on your hips. Relax! You're so stiff.'

'Trrr-rot!'

Cassata lurched into a trot.

'Oh no!' Jenna cried, grabbing at the pommel again.

'Let go! Horizontal arms, like a plane.'

Jenna let go. But she was so nervous she'd forgotten all about her seat. She bounced up and down hard in the saddle. I winced on her behalf, hoping I'd put the icepack back in the freezer.

'Focus, Jenna! You're bouncing all over the saddle like a sack of potatoes. Sit deep. Sit deep!'

'Take it easy, Ash.' A voice came from behind me. I twisted around. Dad was leaning up against a tree.

'What?'

Dad gave me a small smile. He was still in his hospital uniform and looked tired.

Cassata, aware I was distracted, came to a halt and began tearing at the grass. Jenna wasted no time in slipping to the ground.

'I'm no expert,' Dad said. 'But I think you may be expecting too much of Jenna.'

I was shocked. 'What do you mean?'

'Horse riding is new to her. Try and imagine yourself in her shoes.' He smiled. 'In her boots, at least. I seem to remember that it was at least two years after you started lessons at South Beach Stables before you saw a lunge line and that first time you were terrified.'

My mouth dropped open. 'I was?'

It was so long ago. I thought I'd always been on a lunge. I thought it came naturally. Not just to me, to everyone.

Dad joined me and gave me a quick cuddle. 'I know you want Jenna to love horses as much as you do. You've always wanted that. But being best friends doesn't mean you have to like the same things or even be good at the same things. It's your differences that make you so good for each other.'

'I ... I,' I began. 'I just want her to understand what it's like. To ride, to ...' How could I explain it to him? There was no explaining it. It was something that had to happen to you. Flying on horseback. That feeling of not being aware where you end and the horse begins. Was I wrong to want to share it?

'I know, Ash,' Dad said. He gave me another squeeze. 'I know.'

Dad took himself to bed to sleep off the night shift. Jenna and I untacked, cooled down and turned out Cassata. Then we sat down side by side, not talking, not doing anything. Just being together. And for a while I wasn't sure where she ended and I began. There's no explaining it. It's something that just has to happen to you.

THIRTEEN
Money, Money, Money

The next Sunday morning was Jenna's first-ever time at Riding Club. She had joined as a temporary member and even had her own blue Shady Creek Riding Club shirt. I was so proud riding in together on our horses. I felt I would burst. All eyes were on her and most were friendly. Julie and Jodie broke into an enormous grin and waved. Naturally, the Creepketeers did their best to bore holes into her skull with their eyes but I'd warned her to expect nothing less — they were as friendly as funnel-web spiders.

I scanned the faces for Becky and found her sitting alone on a log. She met my eyes and gave me a weak smile. After the training session I'd missed, I'd snuck into Dad's office while Jenna was watching TV and called her, terrified she wasn't speaking to me. I'd said I was sorry over and over again and she'd promised me we were still best friends, but I couldn't help worrying. Something had come between us now. I couldn't really describe it, but I could feel it growing with every day that Jenna stayed in Shady Creek.

We tied Honey and Cassata in the corral and joined Becky on her log. She shuffled up to make room, but we were still pretty squashed. I couldn't help but notice that the Creeps had plenty of room — no one wanted to sit anywhere near them!

Every single member of Shady Creek Riding Club sat under the trees in our 'outdoor clubhouse', squinting up at Gary who looked like he'd smeared a thick coat of black boot polish under each of his eyes. Becky whispered that he'd been in a foul mood all morning and had spent most of the night before lying awake, stressing about the Championships.

'As you guys know, our Riding Club is sponsoring Carly and Becky this year at the Waratah Grove Junior

Cross-Country Riding Championships,' he said once the chatter died down.

Carly made a loud choking noise.

'What's up, Carly? Swallowed a fly?' I said, unable to resist.

'Wouldn't make much of a change from her usual diet,' Jenna whispered. The three of us collapsed in giggles. I was pleased Jenna had been able to make Becky laugh.

Carly looked murderous, but managed to behave in front of Gary. There was no way she wanted to lose that rep spot.

'That means their transport, entry fees and accommodation will be covered,' Gary continued.

I turned slightly to check out Flea and Ryan. Their heads were together. Carly was glaring so hard at Jenna I wouldn't have been surprised if laser beams had shot out of her eyes.

'We've done okay so far. Ash and Becky raised almost eighty dollars from their horseshoe drive and Julie and Jodie's horse wash made buckets of cash.' Gary grinned, waiting for us to laugh at his rotten joke. There was silence. Becky shrank into the log.

'There are plenty of things to come, like our cake stall this afternoon,' Gary continued, hooking his thumbs in the pockets of his jeans. 'But we, I mean *you*, still need to do some serious fundraising.'

The Shady Creek riders moaned collectively.

'We need to organise something that will make us heaps of money very quickly. So I'll leave you to it. I want a brilliant idea from you lot by the end of this meeting.' Gary disappeared into the office, closing the door behind him.

'Ask Ash,' Becky said instantly. 'She's the expert at fundraising.'

'Huh?' I said. I was all wrapped up in a daydream about a hairy, eight-legged Carly sitting on a web, eating flies for dessert.

'You,' said Becky. 'And fundraising.'

'Oh!' I nodded. 'There are heaps of things you can do to make money.' I had tried just about everything to build up my Horse Cents fund, from washing cars to making ribbon browbands to selling off my parents' most prized possessions in a garage sale (Dad *still* brings that up).

'Well, we're not interested in your pathetic ideas, Spiller,' said Carly. 'Those browbands of yours stink.'

'That's not what my many happy customers think, Carly,' I snapped. 'Anyway, if you're so smart, you come up with an idea.'

Carly smiled sweetly and fluttered her eyelashes. 'Already have.' She paused dramatically. 'A beauty pageant.'

'Yuck!' yelled Julie and Jodie the identical twins in unison. Even Flea pretended to vomit into an invisible bucket.

'I know,' said Ryan. 'We could sell horse manure. Five bucks a bag or bag it yourself for two.'

'Who's gonna buy manure around here?' said Becky. 'There are horses all over Shady Creek.'

'What do you suggest we sell?' snapped Carly. 'Dim sims?'

'That's brilliant!' I said, clicking my fingers. 'We could raffle off a dinner for two at Rebecca's Garden.'

For once Carly was gobsmacked. It was the least of her wishes that one of her nasty remarks would make Becky into a hero instead of a zero.

'Not bad,' said Jodie. 'But not enough. And Beck'd have to talk her mum and dad into it.'

Becky smiled and rubbed her hands together, more like her old self than she had been in a week. 'That should be easy.'

'How about selling blackberries? You know, to make jam and stuff. There's heaps around here,' said Flea with a malevolent grin.

'Tell me about it,' I shuddered, remembering my fall from Scud.

'But people pick their own whenever they want them,' moaned Julie. 'And who wants to make jam when you can buy it from the shop?'

'My mum does,' Flea said, sounding annoyed.

'I've got an idea,' said Jenna so quietly it was almost a whisper. 'How about having a dance party?'

'No way!'

'That's even worse than the beauty pageant idea.'

'It makes selling horse poo look good.'

'We might as well just give up!'

Flea stood up. 'Wait a minute, you lot,' he said. 'Jenna's idea is unreal. The best one so far.'

Becky and I stared at each other in utter disbelief. Flea, sticking up for Jenna, in public?

'She has no right to be here,' Carly spat. 'She's not a real member and is only borrowing that fat horse.'

'Don't you dare say that about Cassata,' Becky yelled, jumping to her feet.

'I'll say whatever I like, Rebecca's Garden. I don't care who your daddy is, you can't tell me what to do!'

'Just shut up, Carly. I'm sick of you, d'ya hear me? Sick of you!' Becky was screeching now. I was stunned. I'd never seen her so upset before. I knew she loved her horses and couldn't bear anybody criticising them. But Carly wasn't worth it. I glanced at Gary's office wondering if he'd suddenly developed hearing loss.

Jenna nudged me in the ribs. 'Let's get out of here,' she whispered. 'Before there's trouble.'

'No,' I hissed. 'We can't leave Becky alone.'

Becky was red-faced and trembling. Carly looked very pleased with herself.

'If this is how you deal with pressure, I can't wait to see you trip around the course at Waratah Grove,' Carly sneered at Becky. 'It will be such a pleasure to beat you in a contest that isn't rigged.'

Becky opened her mouth, ready to scream. I grabbed her hand and pulled her down onto the log.

'Forget her,' I said. 'Nobody listens to her.'

I was trying to make her feel better but I didn't believe the words myself. There were plenty of people who listened to Carly and plenty more who did whatever she said no matter how much they disliked her.

'Knock it off,' Flea barked. 'All your ideas suck. I vote for a dance party.'

Carly opened and closed her mouth a few times, looking very much like a cane toad. She thought better of saying whatever she wanted to say and pursed her lips.

'Fine,' I said once the shock of Flea's uncharacteristic decency had worn off. 'A dance party it is. Theme?'

'Horses!' yelled Julie and Jodie and everyone (except Carly, of course) cheered.

FOURTEEN
Runaway Horses

Jenna and I lay on my bedroom floor on our stomachs surrounded by pieces of cardboard and coloured textas.

'There's so much to organise for this dance,' she groaned. 'It's a nightmare.'

I giggled. 'Maybe next time you should keep your brilliant ideas to yourself.'

Jenna outlined a letter 'C' in bright red ink. 'This brings back memories. Seems like only yesterday we were in your room at home racking our brains for Horse Cents.'

'So what's left to do?' I reached across her and grabbed a silver glitter pen; perfect for the horseshoes

I'd decorated my poster with. We were planning to advertise the dance party all over Shady Creek and had been making posters since the last Riding Club meeting. There was about a week to go until the big night and Becky, Jenna and I had been flat out working on our assigned task — promotions and sales.

'Not much,' Jenna said, sounding a little exasperated. 'We just have to make about a thousand posters and put them up all over Shady Creek! And we have to sell tickets. We have to make them too.'

'I'm so glad Gary gave everyone a job.' I set down my pen and began ticking things off on my hands. 'Julie and Jodie are organising the music. Sandra from the Under Tens is bringing drinks from her mum's shop and Flea's mum's making scones with blackberry jam and cream for dessert.'

'Carly should have offered to help,' Jenna scowled. 'It is for her after all.'

'Don't remind me,' I said, feeling real physical pain. 'But you should know her well enough by now to know that helping out isn't one of her strong points. Anyway, we weren't talking about Carly, we were talking about what we still need to do for the dance.' I checked off on my fingers again. 'You are going to use your skills as a computer head to make the tickets and once they're printed we can sell them at Rebecca's Garden. So relax!'

We worked in silence for a while, each of us wrapped in our own thoughts. The dance party was shaping up to be the biggest event the town was going to see all year. The football club (which was run by one of Gary's best mates) had donated the use of its hall, which had its very own sound system. And thanks to a lot of sweet-talking from Becky, other donations were rolling in. Gavin our local butcher was happy to make five hundred sausages for us in return for free advertising. And most of the Shady Creek Riding Club parents had volunteered to do something, whether it was sizzle the sausages on the night or donate prizes for the raffle. So far there was dinner for two at Rebecca's Garden, that tank full of petrol from Ryan and a leg wax from Carly's mum on offer. Just on raffle sales so far, we'd already made enough money to cover one entry fee.

'Jenna?' I said after a while.

'Hmmm?' Jenna was frowning at her poster. She'd left the 'N' out of 'dance' and it now read *Dace Party Saturday Night.*

'There's something I need to tell you.'

Jenna put down her texta. 'What are you talking about?'

I sighed. This holiday wasn't turning out anything like I'd hoped. All my dreams of Jenna, Becky and me riding together and having an amazing time had almost died. Time was running out and I was getting impatient. Jenna was leaving a week after the Championships and if she and Becky weren't going to click on their own, I figured it was up to me to help the situation along. Even if I had to use force.

'Well?' Jenna said, her face serious.

I focussed on my poster and drew a slow, careful balloon with a fat blue texta. 'Becky's coming over soon.'

'So? She comes over all the time.'

'She's sleeping over tonight.' I said the words as fast as I could.

'Oh.'

'It's going to be so cool.' I rubbed my hands together, hoping my enthusiasm would rub off on Jenna. 'We'll ride all afternoon, talk horses all night, watch the greatest horse flicks of all time and ride again in the morning.'

I wanted this sleepover to happen so badly. We should have had a dozen by now, but I'd had to wait until Becky and Jenna started to get along better. And since it was looking like that would never happen I'd decided the time had come to take matters into my own hands. I was positive this sleepover would bring them closer together than ever and that by the end of the summer holidays the three of us would be lifelong best friends and whether or not Jenna became a horse freak wouldn't make any difference.

'Which flicks would they be?'

'*National Velvet, International Velvet, Intergalactic Velvet.* You can't tell me you've never wanted to see them!'

'Ashleigh,' Jenna said, her eyes serious. 'I have some news.'

I sat up quickly, worried. 'What is it? What's wrong?'

Jenna took a deep breath. 'I have never, ever wanted to see *National Velvet*.'

I clutched my chest in mock horror. 'Not even *International Velvet*?'

She laid the back of her hand across her forehead and batted her eyes melodramatically. 'Not even.'

I grabbed my pillow and threw it at her. 'You're nuts!'

She laughed and threw it back, sending my textas flying in all directions.

'But, Ash,' she said, 'are you sure this is a good idea? I don't know if you've noticed, but Becky doesn't seem to like me very much.'

Of course I'd noticed. I'd just been avoiding the subject as best I could for the past week.

'Are you crazy?' I said. 'She loves you! And she hasn't stopped nagging me about having this sleepover.'

I admit it — I exaggerated just a bit. Okay, so I exaggerated a lot. But they were my two best friends and if it was the last thing I did I had to make them like each other.

Jenna regarded me with suspicious blue eyes. 'I've known you since you were five years old and I know when you're up to something, Ashleigh Louise.'

I pulled a face. 'You sound like Mum!'

We dissolved into giggles, only coming to our senses when we heard a faint tapping noise. Becky was standing in the doorway; her school bag in one hand, riding helmet in the other and a look on her face like someone had just told her Carly had been made President of Shady Creek Riding Club.

'How long have you been there?' I said, scrambling to my feet. I dusted myself off, feeling like I'd been caught in the middle of doing something really naughty.

Becky looked from my bed to Jenna's. 'Where should I put my stuff?'

I slapped my hand over my mouth. 'The folding bed! I forgot to put it up. Help me, will you, Jen?'

Jenna got up and smiled awkwardly at Becky. They hadn't had a lot to say to each other since the Riding Club meeting. I had the feeling that although Becky was the last person in the universe who would ever see eye to eye with Carly, neither of them were crazy about Jenna thinking up the idea for the dance.

The three of us set up Becky's bed in the middle of the room and after a quick raid of the fridge set off on a trail ride. It had to work. As we rode out of the driveway together I sent up a quick prayer to the horse gods. This ride had to bring them together. I had run out of ideas and almost run out of time.

★ ★ ★

It was so good to be on a trail ride. Just what I needed. I swiped at a branch and pulled off some gum leaves. Honey ambled along the roadside to my place, followed by Becky on Charlie and Jenna on Cassata. It had been a gorgeous summer afternoon. We had taken Jenna down an easy trail by the creek where there were no jumps, no steep slopes and no surprises. All she'd had to do was sit there and look at the scenery. Cassata was on autopilot as usual.

'I could get used to that,' Jenna mused. 'That kind of riding I like. You can forget all those rules about where to hold my hands and leg aids, though. And lunging was the worst.'

We rode the horses into the corral, untacked them and turned them out to graze.

'How was training?' I asked Becky as we sat down in the paddock to watch the horses. She lay back on the grass and rubbed her eyes.

'Awful. Terrible. Carly is making my life a misery. She criticises everything I do. If Dad tells her to lay off me, she'll be even more convinced I get special treatment.'

The more I thought about it, the happier I was not to have been selected. Becky was a ball of stress.

'The best thing to do is to beat her,' Jenna said thoughtfully. 'If you beat her at the Championships, where your dad and the club have nothing to do with the judging, she'll have to drop the whole thing.'

Becky sat up and nodded. I pulled a twig out of her long thick braid. My stomach growled. None of us had eaten since our snack.

We hauled each other up and wandered inside. Dad was fixing dinner in the kitchen.

'Where's Mum?' I asked, helping myself to three cans of soft drink and a jumbo bag of corn chips.

'Having a lie-down,' he said. 'Girls, would you mind? I need to have a quiet word with Ashleigh.'

I passed everything to Jenna and she and Becky went upstairs to my room. Dad peered around the corner to make sure they were gone.

'What's up?' I said, picking up a baby tomato and popping it into my mouth. I always eat when I'm nervous. And right then I was very nervous. What if Becky was asking Jenna about her family? What if Jenna was crying? What if, worse still, they didn't speak at all?

'How's it going with those two?'

I swallowed my tomato. 'Not too bad.'

'Hmmm.' He leant against the fridge and scratched his chin. 'Why do I get the feeling you're glossing over the facts?'

I shook my head, grabbing a piece of raw carrot. 'Dunno.'

Dad tousled my hair. 'Don't be afraid to come to me and Mum. We know things have been a bit strange.'

'Everything'll be okay. Trust me.'

Dad frowned and picked up his knife. 'Why do I feel nervous every time I hear you say that?'

'Why does everyone say that whenever I say, "trust me"?' I grabbed a handful of salty peanuts from the bowl on the table and bolted up the stairs.

The next morning I was woken early by a horrible scream. I sat straight up in bed. The sun was just beginning to creep through the windows. Jenna rolled over but slept on. Becky's fold-up bed was empty.

The door flew open. Becky stood there in the doorway in her pyjamas. Her hair was tangled around her face like a web.

'They're gone!' she said.

'Who?'

'The horses! They're gone!'

I leapt out of bed and raced to the window. 'You're joking!'

'Of course I'm not! See for yourself.'

Becky leant over Jenna and shook her. Jenna rubbed her eyes and yawned.

'What? What's the matter?'

'The horses are gone,' I said, pulling my boots on. 'I'm going to look for them.'

'Like that?' Jenna asked, sitting up.

I looked down at my nightie. It was old, but my favourite. Ages ago I'd ironed a gorgeous transfer of a chestnut Arab on the front. 'I don't care how we look. Who's with me?'

'Me,' Becky said, wrestling her hair into a messy ponytail. 'Jenna?'

'Shouldn't we get dressed?'

Becky's eyes widened. 'Are you mad? They could be miles away by then.'

Becky and I raced for the door. Jenna followed, pulling on her joggers.

'How could they have gotten out?' I said as we ran down the stairs and out of the back door. I could hear Mum crashing about in the kitchen. The smell of toast was everywhere. 'Who closed the gate last night?'

Becky rubbed her forehead with her hands as we scanned the empty paddock. 'You filled the water trough, I gave them a feed. Jenna, what did you do?'

Jenna's face drained of colour. 'I closed the gate.'

Becky groaned. 'You mustn't have shut it properly. Look what you've done!'

Tears welled in Jenna's eyes. She had been so upset by her parents' divorce that it didn't take much to make her cry. I was sure if Becky had known she'd have tried a lot harder to bite her tongue.

'I'm sorry,' Jenna said through streams of tears. 'I thought it was closed.'

I pulled on Jenna's hand. 'Don't worry. It was a mistake. It could happen to anyone.'

'Well it shouldn't have happened!' Becky whined.

'Give her a break,' I said. 'Jenna's new to this whole horse thing. I should have shut the gate.'

Becky burst into tears. 'You always take her side.'

She ran down the driveway and down the road towards Riding Club. There was a good chance they'd be there. It was like their second home.

I wanted to follow her, but again I found myself being torn in two. There was no sense in all three of us going in the same direction. We'd find the horses much faster if we split up and I couldn't send Jenna off by herself. So Jenna and I ran together, the other way.

As we zipped past Flea's house, I thought I saw the curtain move. 'Great,' I said. 'All I need is for Flea to see me in my nightie and riding boots.'

I expected Jenna to laugh, but she was crying. She looked such a mess, jogging down the road in her pyjamas with her nose running and tears spilling down her face.

'They'll turn up, Jen. There isn't a horse owner around who hasn't had to go horse hunting at the crack of dawn before. There! I see them.'

They were on the corner of the street, grazing contentedly. It only took a minute to reach them. I took a handful of Honey's mane with one hand (scolding her for giving me such a fright) and grabbed Charlie's halter with the other. Jenna took hold of Cassata's and we led them home.

Becky had seen us and was waiting, her face blotchy. She snatched Charlie and Cassata's halters. 'I'm taking them home.'

Jenna looked at the ground. I knew she was willing herself not to start crying again.

'One more chance, Becky,' I said. 'Just wait until after the Championships.'

Becky said nothing. She marched down the road in her pyjamas, leading Charlie and Cassata behind her. My sleepover was finished.

FIFTEEN

Kick Up Your Hooves

The week after the disastrous sleepover was busy with last-minute things to do for the dance. There were ticket sales to tally, emergency Riding Club meetings and even a spot on the local radio station's 'What's on this Week in the Creek' segment that Gary had managed to tee up. And then there were the regular school holiday things that simply had to be done, like swimming in the pool with Jenna, putting away the Christmas tree for Mum (for two dollars each) and taking Honey and Cassata on long trail rides all over Shady Creek.

Becky had been made to return Cassata almost as soon as she had taken her home, once she had changed out of her pyjamas. Gary had called Mum and Dad to apologise and on the surface things had been smoothed over. But as is usually the case, just because the surface is smooth does not mean that things beneath it are calm.

I didn't see much of Becky at all that week. She was always at training or resting at home and I was so preoccupied with Jenna and our horses that when the Saturday of the dance arrived it almost took me by surprise.

Jenna and I arrived at the footy club hall early. It was barely recognisable. A huge mirror ball hung from the ceiling, hay bales, saddles and bridles were scattered everywhere in keeping with the horsy theme, and the leftover horseshoes that Becky and I had decorated were hanging over the double doors (now that their job on our Christmas trees was well and truly over for the year). Jenna gaped at the decorations. She looked stunning with her blonde hair braided into an elegant crown around her head and fluorescent pink elastic bands on her braces. Almost every member of Shady Creek Riding Club was there ready to help. Gary was running all over the place like a manic miniature pony, making a lot of noise but not achieving very much. Mrs Cho was spreading out the food on the tables. There were trays piled high with fried rice and noodles, steaming chicken and beef dishes with spicy sauces and what seemed like thousands of spring rolls and dim sims. It all looked so good! I had to drag Jenna away so that we could drool over the other tables, which were just as tempting — donuts, lamingtons, drinks, ice creams, cherries, mangoes, nectarines, watermelon! And to top it all off, a team of Riding Club parents were sizzling sausages, steak and onions on a gigantic barbecue. I couldn't wait to start eating. But first there was some dancing to do. And dance we did! It would all have been perfect if there hadn't been so much tension between Becky and Jenna.

They had barely said hello to one another and were doing a great job of making it clear to everyone in Shady Creek that there was trouble in paradise. Instead of dancing together and having the best time, Becky and Jenna had installed themselves at opposite ends of the hall and had me running between them.

Carly, always quick to sniff out a fight, sidled up to me and sneered, regarding me through thick black eye make-up. 'Your little city friend is a gem. We're loving every minute of watching Rebecca's Garden squirm. Can you talk Jenny into moving here for good?'

I cupped my hand around my ear although I'd heard every word. 'Can't hear you,' I shouted. 'Music's too loud.'

I edged away from her and tried to slip into the crowd of dancers. She followed me, as keen to torture me as a cat toying with a lizard it's about to eat.

'I can't figure out why everyone wasted their time organising this dance.' She looked around the hall at the flashing lights, the food, the people dancing and the giant cardboard horseshoe which leant against the wall marking how much money had been raised. So far it was two-thirds coloured in. 'Gary's little favourite going to Waratah Grove is a waste of an entry fee. Besides, if she knows what's best for her she'll stay away.'

I stared at Carly, stunned. 'Is that a threat?'

Carly shrugged, flicking her red hair over her shoulder as she sauntered away. 'Take it however you like it, Spiller.'

Becky pushed through the crowd and grabbed my arm. 'What did she want?'

I shook my head, not really knowing what to say. Becky was nervous enough about Waratah Grove — I figured the fewer threats she heard from Carly, the better off she'd be. 'Not much. She was just going on about the food.'

I craned over the crowd to catch a glimpse of Carly, Flea and Ryan, their heads together. Every now and then they sent horrible looks in our direction.

'I wish they hadn't come,' Becky moaned. 'They ruin everything.'

I was tempted to point out that there were two other people doing a great job of ruining the dance, but clamped my mouth shut.

'Coming to training tomorrow?' Becky shouted over the music.

'Maybe,' I yelled. 'It depends.'

'On what?' Becky frowned. I'd missed most of her training sessions since Jenna had arrived and I knew it bothered her, but Jenna wasn't interested in watching Becky train.

I avoided Becky's dark eyes on purpose, not wanting to see the pain I knew I was causing her. 'It depends on Jenna.'

Becky rolled her eyes and put her drink down on the nearest table. 'I should have known.'

'She's got less than two weeks left in Shady Creek,' I said. 'Can't we meet up later for a trail ride instead? Jenna really likes trail rides.'

Becky shrugged. 'Whatever.'

I squeezed her hand. 'C'mon, Beck. You know I'd be there if I could. I'll be there in spirit.'

Becky looked into my eyes. Something terrible had happened to hers. They were dull, sad and they'd lost the sparkle I'd come to love so much. 'It doesn't matter. I'll just see you after.'

'Great!' I said, trying to sound as cheerful as I could. 'I can't wait.'

Becky gave me a small, tight smile, turned away and made a beeline for Gary who was busy colouring in the rest of his cardboard horseshoe. As he finished he started shouting that we'd made enough money not only to cover the two entry fees, but enough to hire a bus to transport Riding Club members to the Championships to cheer on Becky and Carly.

The dance had been a hit and I should have been feeling on top of the world. Instead, I felt miserable. I scanned the room for Jenna and spotted her standing between Julie and Jodie, looking through a box of CDs. She saw me and waved, a huge grin on her face. I waved back and for a moment things didn't seem so bad. Until, that is, I met Becky's eyes and at that moment I realised I was in danger of losing her. Nothing had ever been more scary.

SIXTEEN

Trailblazers

Jenna and I followed Becky down a narrow path that had been cut through the thick trees especially for horse riding. The sun was beating down on us and there was a strong wind whipping at our faces, and thrashing the branches of what seemed like thousands of trees on either side of the path. I wished it would bring some relief from the heat, but it only made things hotter. I couldn't help wishing there was something bringing relief from the tension between Jenna and Becky. I didn't feel comfortable when they were together any more, especially that morning. Since we'd met up about an hour earlier, hardly a word had been spoken. It had been my idea to go on this trail ride, despite the rotten weather. In my heart I hoped it would somehow fix everything. My head told me otherwise.

I flicked a handful of Honey's golden mane over her shoulder. The wind tossed it back again.

'Let's sing!' I said, desperate to break the terrible silence between us.

Becky gave me a look.

'C'mon, it'll be fun. And it'll keep the bunyips away.'

'Ash-leigh!' Jenna whined. She squinted and rubbed at her eyes as a cloud of grit and dust blew up into her face.

I launched into 'Waltzing Matilda', undeterred. Jenna joined in.

'Don't you think you should be concentrating? Especially on a day like this,' Becky said loudly, over the top of verse two. She didn't seem to be enjoying our trail ride karaoke one little bit.

It's true that Jenna wasn't riding well, holding onto her pommel and allowing her reins to slacken. But she was enjoying herself in the saddle and as far as I was concerned that was the main thing. Cassata was like a ship without a captain though, cruising along at her own pace. She followed Charlie closely with her nose to his tail.

'Watch it!' Becky grouched. 'You'll clip Charlie's heels. I'm going to Waratah Grove in a week.'

Jenna pulled on Cassata's reins. The Appaloosa stopped dead as a sudden gust of scorching wind blew her mane up straight like a zebra's. I would have laughed if it hadn't been for the look on Becky's face as she twisted around in the saddle.

'Not so hard! You'll hurt her.'

I pulled Honey up beside Cassata, frustration welling up inside me. 'She only did what you asked her to.'

Becky's eyes moistened.

'You always take her side!' she said.

'No, I don't.'

'You've been like this all holiday. I can't say anything without you sticking up for Jenna, even when she's doing the wrong thing.' Becky was crying now. Tears streamed down her face. She wiped at her nose with the back of her riding glove. Although her tears seemed to have come from nowhere I knew she'd been upset since the sleepover.

'But, Becky,' I began. I glanced at Jenna who was staring at the ground, red-faced. 'Things have been hard for Jenna this year.'

'So you keep saying.' Becky tightened her grip on her reins as Charlie spun in a sudden circle. He tossed his head, unsettled by the wind, which stirred crisp, dry leaves around his legs.

Jenna's eyes widened. 'What have you told her?'

'Nothing!' I said. My heart beat a little faster. 'I haven't said a word.'

'See,' Becky sobbed. 'You're still keeping secrets from me. Some friend you've turned out to be!'

'I am your friend. I'm your best friend.' My heart was beating so hard now that blood pumped in my ears. I could hear it over the wind and the crashing of the branches and leaves and the shrieking parrots and everything else. I stroked Honey's neck, trying to calm myself down.

'No, you're not!' Becky cried. She pointed at Jenna. 'You're her best friend. Rachael was right for once. Three is a crowd.'

'That's not fair!' I said. 'We can all be best friends. The three of us.' Honey danced on her forelegs. Only Cassata was calm.

'No,' Becky said, shaking her head emphatically. 'We can't. Best friends don't keep secrets from each other.'

I opened my mouth, but there was nothing I could say. Becky was right.

'I thought you were different but you're just like the Creeps. I wish I'd never met you, Ashleigh. I wish you'd never come to Shady Creek!'

'I can't believe you're saying this.' Tears welled in my eyes. My throat tightened and I knew I was going to cry as well. I felt sick.

Becky gathered her reins and kicked Charlie hard. I'd never seen her kick him like that before. She yelled over her shoulder at us to drop dead as she cantered away.

'Becky, wait!' I called after her, but it was too late. She had already disappeared into the bush. I couldn't follow her. I couldn't leave Jenna alone. I stared down the track for a moment, not sure what to do next, tears spilling down my face.

'We should get out of here,' I muttered to Jenna. She had been very quiet. I'd almost forgotten she was still there.

'This is all my fault.'

'No.' I shook my head, gulping at my tears. I leant over, patting Jenna's knee. 'It's mine.'

'I'm sorry for everything. I should never have come here.' Jenna's voice was small. She twisted Cassata's mane around her fingers.

I shook my head again. 'Don't say that. I wanted you to come. We've been friends since …'

'Forever?' Jenna gave me a weak smile.

'Forever.' I held out my hand and she clasped it. 'Don't worry. We'll go after Becky and when we find her we can sort this whole mess out.'

'And I'll tell her about my parents. I should never have asked you to keep it a secret.' Jenna sighed. 'Everyone's gonna know about it soon anyway.'

A branch whipped against my face out of the blue. I ducked, too late. I touched my cheek and looked at my fingertips. Blood. It started to sting and I suddenly realised something the horses had known for the last fifteen minutes. The weather had gone crazy.

'Are you okay?' Jenna said.

I nodded. 'Yeah.'

The trees were bending almost double in the wind. Their branches were cracking, the noise ringing out like shots. Honey pawed at the ground, urging me to move on.

'I think we should get out of here!' I shouted. 'It's too dangerous for the horses.'

'And us!' Jenna agreed.

I looked down the trail, thinking for a moment, trying to figure out what to do. I was still fairly new in Shady Creek and I'd only been down this trail a couple of times. I needed Becky to show me how to get out. My heart squeezed as I thought about her. I realised then what a good friend she was, how she had looked after me from my first day at Shady Creek Primary School. How she'd been there for me and for Honey no matter what. I realised how much I had let her down. I'd been so caught up with Jenna and her problems that I'd pushed Becky aside. She was right. Some friend I'd turned out to be.

'C'mon, Ash,' Jenna said. 'I'm not enjoying this.'

I shook my head and stared all around me. The branches thrashed together, like huge green and brown pompoms shaking and shaking, out of control.

'This way,' I said, urging Honey down the track at a trot, the same way Becky had gone. Following her seemed the only sensible thing to do.

'Shouldn't we just turn around?' Jenna called out from behind me. She was managing a jerky rising trot.

'There's no point. This trail is sort of like a horseshoe. It comes out a bit down the road from where we started and we're already more than halfway. If we turn back it'll take us twice as long to get out.'

'What's that stuff?' Jenna yelled.

I twisted around. 'What?'

Jenna pointed upwards at a trickle of what looked like black raindrops. I caught one in my hand. It was an ember.

'Jenna, we have to get out of here!'

'What's wrong?'

'You need to canter,' I cried. 'Just trust me, okay?'

'I can't canter!'

'Jenna, you have to try.' I was pleading now. Sweat broke out on my forehead and ran down my cheeks. Tiny black embers fell all around us. I sniffed at the air. Smoke. Faint, but there was no doubt about it. It clicked then. The wind, the heat, the birds going mad. There was a fire.

'Can you smell something?' Jenna called.

I didn't want to panic her. 'Maybe someone's having a barbecue.'

'In the middle of the bush? In this gale?'

I looked behind me. Jenna was scared. Her face and lips were pale.

'Don't lie to me, Ash. We're in trouble, aren't we?'

I nodded. Jenna burst into tears.

The smell became stronger and the air grew hazy. The wind was so strong now it felt like riding through something solid, like jelly — hot, sticky, smoky jelly. Honey was wound up, scared. She held her head high and tight, desperate to gallop away. I kept her reined in, forcing her to trot, the only pace Jenna was comfortable with other than a walk. I cursed myself, wishing that I'd made her stick at her riding lessons.

There was a crash on my right and Honey lurched sideways, shying. Some kangaroos bounded out of the trees onto the trail and down the track in the direction we had just come.

'We must be riding towards it,' I said, feeling panic rise inside me.

Jenna pulled Cassata up. She was crying hard. 'I told you. We have to turn around.'

She was right. It was our only choice. I swung Honey around and coughed. The air was growing thick with grey smoke. My eyes watered. I could hear the snapping of branches and the crunching of leaves as animals made their escape.

'Jenna, stop!' I called, as she turned Cassata back down the track. 'Becky!'

Jenna's face fell. 'She must have gotten out by now. She's a good rider.'

I shook my head. 'We can't leave without making sure she's okay. We have to go looking for her. Ouch!'

I looked down at my arm. An ember, still glowing, had burnt my skin. I brushed it off, and rubbed at the sore. More fell from the sky.

'Are you crazy?' Jenna shrieked.

It was getting worse. Tiny fragments of hot charred black leaves swirled around us, settling on our helmets and in the horses' manes. They stung our hands and faces. The horses stamped and whinnied in fright, tugging at their bits, begging us to order them on to safety. I'd never seen Cassata unsettled before. She'd always been as quiet as a rocking horse.

'She's my friend. We're not leaving without her.'

Jenna turned Cassata around and followed me grimly into the smoke, her T-shirt pulled up over her nose. The smoke was in my eyes, my nose, my mouth, my throat. I could taste it.

'Jenna, you have to go faster. You have to canter,' I yelled, more frightened than ever. My teeth were chattering.

'I can't, I can't!' she cried.

I looked over my shoulder. Jenna's face was dusty and streaked with tears.

'Look!' I pointed at a small spot fire, burning just a few metres away.

'Oh no!' Jenna sobbed.

'You have to trust me! You have to trust Cassata!' I squeezed my legs against Honey's sides and she stretched into a canter, pleased I was allowing her her head at last. Cassata followed suit. Jenna screamed. I glanced at her over my shoulder. She was clinging to the pommel hard. We cantered down the track, swooping under low hanging branches and dodging fallen logs.

'Becky!' I called, then coughed uncontrollably. 'Becky!'

I heard a scream and pushed Honey on. Honey shook her head, rolling her eyes. Her ears were laid back and she snorted in terror.

'Just a bit further,' I assured her, clutching a handful of her mane, pushing the fear deep down. Fear that we'd meet the fire face to face. Fear that we wouldn't find Becky. Fear that by pushing Honey on, I was putting her life at risk.

It wasn't long before I saw what looked through the smoke like a pile of crumpled rags with a tangled web of thick black hair lying on the track ahead of us. I pulled Honey up and dropped to the ground, rushed forward and crouched over Becky. My eyes stung. I coughed again.

Becky looked up at me. Her face was scratched and bleeding. She moaned. Tears had cut streaks through the dirt on her cheeks. Her hair was a mess of sticks and leaves and her riding clothes were torn. She must have taken a terrible fall.

'Ashleigh!' she croaked. 'Jenna! Thank goodness. I was so scared.'

'We've got to get out of here!' I pulled her to her feet and she yelped.

'What's wrong?' Jenna called, terrified.

'My ankle hurts,' Becky sobbed. 'And my arm.'

It was bent at a sickening angle. Dark bruises spread across her skin.

'Let's get out of here,' I said, wrapping her good arm around my neck. I helped her limp to Cassata and forced her foot into Jenna's stirrup.

'I can't,' she cried as I pushed her up onto Cassata's back behind Jenna. 'Charlie's spooked. He's gone. I have to find him.'

'I'll find him.'

Jenna's eyes were wide. She was trembling. 'What do I do?'

I swung back into the saddle. 'Turn around. Canter as fast as you can. Get Becky out of here. I'm going to find Charlie.'

'I can't!' Jenna screamed. 'I can't canter by myself.'

'You don't have a choice.' I gathered my reins and wheeled Honey back towards the fire. 'Now go!'

Jenna whimpered, but obeyed. Becky wrapped her good arm around her injured one and sobbed. I watched them canter down the track until they were out of sight knowing every step must be agonising for Becky.

Now I was alone.

But I had a choice. I could gallop for mine and Honey's lives after Jenna and Becky. Or I could push her further down the track, which was veiled in thick smoke and look for Charlie.

'This is it, Honey!' I shouted over the noise of the wind and the crashing, smashing branches, trying hard to convince myself that what I was about to do was sane. But Charlie was Becky's horse and Becky was my best friend. I had to do it.

Honey spun around, determined to tear away after Cassata but I wheeled her around again and drummed at her sides with my heels. She reared suddenly, lashing out with her front hooves at the smoky shadows.

I clung to the saddle, coughing, and pulled my T-shirt over my nose.

'Come on! For me. For Charlie!'

I pushed her forward, crouching low against her neck, squinting, my eyes and nose running. Sweat ran down my back. My hair dripped under my helmet. I clutched at the reins, which slipped through my shaking fingers.

The bush melted into a blur of shapes and sounds. Animals crashed through the trees in terror.

Birds screeched high over our heads. Honey resisted but I pushed her on. Further and further, harder and harder.

'Charlie!' I screamed. 'Char-lie!'

Honey whinnied, high-pitched and desperate. Her cry was answered by the scream of a horse, a sound that made me shiver.

Finally I saw him. Charlie stood just off the track with his reins tangled around a tree. I pulled Honey up and leapt to the ground. Charlie tossed his head and yanked on his reins, rolling his eyes and wheezing in fear.

'Easy,' I said, patting his neck. He was soaked with sweat and coated with white lather. 'What have you done to yourself?'

I pulled at the reins, but they were stuck fast. Charlie pulled back, digging his heels into the ground. The tree groaned, but the reins refused to budge.

Don't panic, I thought. Don't panic, just think. I could take off his bridle. But how would I get him out? He could bolt into the fire and be lost forever. There had to be another way.

I fumbled with each of the buckles that looped around Charlie's bit. Becky kept his reins so supple they unbuckled easily. Within moments Charlie was free, but without reins. They dangled from the tree, useless.

Think, think! I told myself. What should I use? How can I lead him out? Can I trust him to gallop behind us all the way home? He was so spooked. Then I got it.

I held fast to Charlie's bit with one hand and unbuckled my belt with the other, slipping the thin leather through the two loops.

'It's not reins, but it'll do,' I shouted. 'Now let's go.'

Leading Charlie, I mounted Honey, shoving my feet deep into the stirrups. Honey needed no encouragement. We cantered along the track to safety, Charlie by our sides, saved by the belt.

SEVENTEEN

Taking Up the Reins

'You're a hero,' Becky said, looking up at me from her bed at the Shady Creek and Districts Hospital. She had a broken arm and a twisted ankle, but was otherwise okay.

Gary was furious with her, though, in a relieved parent kind of way. According to him, Jenna and I, as city kids, didn't know any better but she, as a born and bred Shady Creeker, should have known bushfire weather when she saw it. My parents weren't thrilled with me either. I'd spent most of last night on the receiving end of a very long lecture about the dangers of the Australian bush, the consequences of reckless behaviour and the utter stupidity of putting my house guest in unnecessary peril. Jenna had gotten off with a brief, albeit hysterical, phone call from her mum.

Jenna nodded. 'You're a total hero.'

I blushed and picked at the crisp white sheet that tucked under Becky's mattress. 'Honey's the real hero. She never gave up on you and Charlie.'

'She loves you,' Becky said. 'She'd do anything for you.'

'Anyway, how about you?' I poked Jenna's arm. 'You *rescued* Becky. That's amazing!'

'Anytime,' she said. 'You really should thank Cassata though.'

'Our two horse heroes. They should get medals.' Becky scratched under her cast with a pen. 'How's Cassata?'

'Strained tendon,' I said softly. I hadn't wanted to bring it up. Becky loved her horses too much to bear it when they were sick or injured.

Becky went pale. 'And Charlie?'

'Smoke inhalation and shock. A few cuts to his legs too. He'll have to be rested for a while.'

Becky lay back into the pillows. 'If I hadn't taken off, if I hadn't acted like such an idiot, none of this would have happened.'

Jenna and I exchanged worried glances. The last thing we'd wanted to do by visiting Becky was stress her out. She needed to relax and recover. Just like her horses. Strictly speaking she wasn't allowed more than one visitor at a time but Dad had sneaked us in. There are some advantages to having a dad who is a nurse.

'You can get better together,' Jenna said as brightly as she could.

Becky smiled at her and sank deeper into her pillows. She and Jenna seemed to be getting along better. I hoped so, at least. Escaping from a raging bushfire on horseback can tend to bring two people closer. At least now they had something in common.

'So what happened yesterday?' Becky said. 'Dad didn't say very much. And Mum nearly had a heart attack so I didn't think I should ask her.'

'Some total morons didn't put out their campfire properly,' I said, rolling my eyes. 'The volunteer fire fighters got it under control pretty quickly, thank goodness.'

'More smoke than flame,' Jenna added.

'Good,' Becky said with a sigh. She chewed on her bottom lip for a moment. 'I need to say something.'

Jenna turned to leave.

'Don't go,' Becky said. 'I want you to hear this, too.'

Jenna took her place by my side again. Becky took a deep breath.

'I'm just so sorry, Ash,' she said.

I frowned, confused. 'For what?'

'For almost ruining your holiday.'

'What?' I gaped at her. 'It's my fault. You were right. I have been just like a Creep.'

Becky pulled a face and we laughed.

'You look like you just smelled something really bad!' I said, waving my hand around under my nose. 'There must be a Creepketeer around.'

'No, it's my fault,' Jenna said. 'I shouldn't have made Ash keep a secret. So I'll tell you right now what it was. My parents are getting divorced. I s'pose by not talking about it I was trying to make it not happen. If you get what I mean.'

Becky nodded. 'I do get it. And I'm so sorry.'

'And I should have tried harder at riding lessons,' Jenna continued. 'And I should have closed the gate properly. And ...'

'Forget about it!' Becky said, smiling. 'It's all over. I was being silly over Ashleigh. Before she came here I was alone. The Creeps turned everyone against me. But Ash stuck by me. When you came to stay I got scared. I didn't want to be alone again.'

I squeezed her hand. 'That will never happen. We are best friends.'

'I know. Only you would have come looking for me. And Charlie.'

We beamed at each other. I was so relieved. It was all over, the fire, the tension, the secrets — everything. I just had one more thing I needed to say. Something I should have said weeks ago.

'Jenna, I'm sorry.'

Jenna looked confused. 'What for now?'

'I pushed you too hard.' I took a deep breath and sighed. I wanted Jenna just the way she was. She didn't have to be as horse mad as me. She didn't have to be horse mad at all. She just had to be herself. 'From now on you only have to be in the saddle when and if you really want to be.'

My voice cracked. Jenna's eyes filled with tears. Becky held out her good arm and the three of us hugged hard.

'How sweet!' said a voice.

We broke apart and smoothed our shirts. Becky went back to scratching under her cast. Jenna stared at the curtain, suddenly finding the pattern of aeroplanes and helicopters intensely interesting.

'What do you want, Carly?' I demanded.

Carly leant against the door to Becky's room and smirked, holding out a withered bunch of red geraniums that looked like they'd been ripped from the hospital's garden. 'I came to wish the patient a speedy recovery. How long will your cast be on?'

Becky stopped scratching long enough to slip Carly a disgusted glance. 'Six weeks,' she muttered.

Carly dropped the geraniums on the bed and slapped her hands to her pasty cheeks, feigning shock. 'Oh, how terrible! The Championships are, oh let me see, a week away. How will you ride over all those big scary obstacles with a broken arm?'

I bristled with fury, wanting to slap Carly's cheeks with my own hands.

'I won't,' Becky spat. 'And the only thing that's keeping me from putting you in this bed is knowing that Ashleigh's gonna beat you for me.'

'Uh,' I wheeled around. 'What are you talking about?'

I knew exactly what she was talking about. I'd known it since the minute I realised Becky wasn't going to Waratah Grove. I just hadn't wanted to say it out loud. It felt like my fault. I thought about all those times I'd dreamt of going to the Championships and how I'd wanted to beat Becky so badly and I felt like I'd thrown her off Charlie myself.

'Carly knows as well as I do. My place has to go to the runner-up. That's you, Ash.'

I swallowed. 'Yeah, I, uh, I know.'

'The one and only Ashleigh Miller.' Carly perched herself on Becky's bed, making her wince.

'I'm calling security,' Becky said, pulling her buzzer down from its peg on the wall above her bed.

'How about a pest exterminator?' Jenna was seething.

'I was just leaving,' Carly said, jumping off the bed as Becky pressed hard on the buzzer. 'But I hope you get out of here soon.'

'That was almost charming, Carly,' I said, indicating the doorway.

Carly grinned wickedly at Becky. 'So you'll be well enough to come and see me whip the joddies off Miller and her nag.'

Then she turned to me, looking into my eyes with all the warmth of an iceberg. 'I'm looking forward to this, Spiller. You have no idea how much.'

Then she disappeared just as a nurse rushed in to wrestle the buzzer from Becky's hand.

Despite Carly being her usual poisonous self and almost ruining another day for me in Shady Creek, my head was spinning. I was going to the Waratah Grove Junior Cross-Country Riding Championships. It was all I'd dreamt of since Gary had first made the announcement at Riding Club. Now that seemed like years ago.

Jenna nudged me. 'Good on you, Ash. You'll do great!'

I chewed on my bottom lip. 'I'm so sorry, Beck.'

Becky shook her head slowly. 'I just can't believe it. All that training. It's all I ever wanted and now ... Dad is so upset.'

That was it.

'I'm not going,' I said. 'No way.'

Becky frowned. 'What are you talking about?'

'I haven't trained. Honey's not ready. I'm not ready.' The guilt I had felt earlier was being washed away by fear. This wasn't Gary's home-made cross-country course. This was Waratah Grove.

'Don't be dumb.'

'I'm going to tell your dad to count me out. I can't do it.'

Becky sat up and grabbed my hand. 'Don't!' she said fiercely. 'You deserve this. You're the only other rider in the whole district who *can* do it. I'm glad it's you. And I know you'll do great.'

'Are you sure?' I searched her eyes.

'I'm positive.' Becky grinned at me, that old sparkle I loved was back.

'Okay,' I said, feeling better. Just a little bit better.

'Do me one favour?' Becky squeezed my hand.

'Anything.'

'Win. You have to beat Carly. If she won …'

I shook my head, squeezing Becky's hand right back. 'The Creeps'll be unbearable. Don't worry, Becky. There must be something we can do.'

'Yeah,' Jenna said, clasping our hands with hers. 'And when we figure out what it is she's history.'

We were united at last. The three of us against the three of them.

EIGHTEEN

Show Off

'So what are your plans for today?' Mum peered at me over her spoonful of mushy bran cereal.

'I've got to get to Riding Club,' I said in between mouthfuls of toast smeared with jam. I took a huge gulp of orange juice, got up from the table and slapped a kiss on her cheek. She wiped away the sticky juice with a paper serviette. 'There are only six days to go until the Championships. That's six: S-I-X!'

'I think I get it.' Mum sipped at a glass of water and looked at her watch.

'No coffee for you?' I asked, grabbing my riding hat from the junk table beside the door.

'I've given it up.'

'Has Jenna already gone to Becky's?' I hadn't seen her all morning.

Mum rinsed her bowl and spoon and stacked them neatly in the sink. 'She left a while ago.'

'Oh.' Becky and Jenna had organised it at the hospital. They'd said they had to strategise. In other words they'd be spending the morning reading the Riding Club rule book from cover to cover, looking for something that would catch Carly out. I hadn't wanted to say it out loud but it was a waste of time. Carly wasn't stupid. She'd make sure she played by the rules on the day. I just hoped she would make a mistake. I didn't say anything to Becky and Jenna, though. They'd only been getting along for twelve hours and I didn't want to get in their way. I jammed my helmet down over my head.

Half an hour later I was cantering Honey in figure eights in the warm-up arena. Carly was in the ring with me but so far we had done an excellent job of ignoring one another. Getting the silent treatment from Carly for once was actually enjoyable. It allowed me to concentrate on other things. Like Honey's gait.

She cantered smoothly beneath me, her hooves hitting the dirt rhythmically. Her ears were pricked forward and alert, her silky golden mane bounced along with her stride. I breathed in all the smells of Shady Creek Riding Club: leather bridles and saddles, horses, dust and trees.

'Morning, you two!' Gary beamed and waved us over to the fence. Bonnie was chewing her breakfast of lucerne hay in the corral. I slowed Honey to a trot, then to a light, springy walk.

'How are you feeling?' Gary's eyes searched my face as I pulled Honey up.

How was I feeling?

Throughout the warm-up, without being able to help myself, I had sneaked looks at Carly and Destiny. They had trained for weeks and were ready for anything Waratah Grove could throw at them. Honey and I, on the other hand, had spent our time going on trail rides, loping around with Jenna and jumping the odd supportive barrel with Becky. I felt we were as unready as could be.

'Good,' I said in a loud voice, hoping volume would disguise my fears. 'Great, in fact.'

Gary nodded and pulled his cap down lower over his eyes. 'With less than a week to go, I'm expecting you two to be here at Riding Club by eight every morning for a two-hour training session.'

'Eight o'clock?' Carly almost choked. 'But it's holidays!'

'It's also summer,' Gary said. 'And I don't know about you, but I don't want to be out here at midday. It's too hot for the horses, not to mention our two star riders.'

Carly sulked, but closed her mouth.

'Both horse and rider must be fit and very well-trained to compete at the level you two will be competing at. So let's get out there!'

Carly wheeled Destiny around and trotted her out of the ring towards the cross-country course, anxious to go first. I noticed a crowd had begun to gather at points around the course.

'Our loyal team of volunteer jump judges are on duty this morning,' Gary said, walking beside Honey and me.

We stopped at the starting line. Carly was waiting, of course, a nasty sneer on her face.

'I guess you're on first, Carly.'

Gary rang a small hand-held bell and Destiny stretched into a canter then sped up to a gallop, Carly keen to use as little time as possible on a straight run. I watched her clear the first jump, the log, then disappear around the corner as I shortened my stirrups two notches.

'Ready?' Gary asked.

'As I'll ever be,' I muttered.

Gary raised the bell into the air and did something to his stopwatch with his thumb. 'Ready, three, two,' he said, ringing the bell loudly on 'ONE!'

Honey flinched at the noise of the bell, but leapt from the starting line like a rabbit. Gary had given Carly a good head start. This wasn't about catching up to her and racing her to the finish line. This was about getting us through the course with no refusals, no falls or mistakes and in a time I could be proud of. It was only about two weeks since I'd ridden the course but it almost felt like the first time. It was probably my imagination, but it even looked different. Red and white flags flapped in the morning breeze.

We neared the first jump.

'Red on my right,' I thought.

Honey surged forward and I reined her in slightly to set her up for the jump. She bore down on the bit and leapt madly over the jump, ignoring my command. My heart pumped half-terrifying, half-delicious adrenaline through my veins.

I heard a voice yell 'clear' as we galloped away.

'Go easy!' I shouted, cursing myself for all the no-rules trail riding we'd been doing instead of training.

Honey relaxed and we soared over one obstacle after another — the wall, the tyres, the barrels — and each time heard the jump judge yell 'clear'. My heart sang as we galloped, the air beating fresh and cool against my face. My Honey and I were one. That feeling was so precious; it was better than anything I knew.

We jumped the post and rails and turned slightly to the right to take the ditch. I gathered up loops of rein and rose in the saddle just as Honey pushed off. I felt her stretch out and land clean on the other side of the ditch.

'Good girl!' I cried, slapping my palm against her neck. Just a few more and we'd be home.

'Fault!'

'What?' I twisted around in the direction of the voice, lost my stirrups and felt myself slip from the saddle. Honey, feeling the sudden shift in weight from her back to her side, halted at once. I hauled myself up into the saddle and shoved my feet back into the stirrups.

'Who said that?' I called, twisting around in the saddle. It had to be a mistake. Honey had cleared the ditch by a mile.

'Fault,' the voice repeated. I spotted a volunteer jump judge in a heavy coat and thick sunglasses leaning against a tree.

Stunned, I wheeled Honey around and rode towards the jump again. She soared, clearing it easily.

'Fault. Move on, rider.'

I couldn't believe it. In competition we'd be eliminated after three faults on the one obstacle. Urging Honey back into a canter towards the next obstacle, my head was spinning. Had I made a mistake? Had Honey's hooves landed clear of the ditch or not? It had happened so fast. I just wanted to have a perfect run. To prove to Gary, Carly and myself that we were up for this.

The rest of the ride was sour, like an opening night nobody has bothered to show up for. Honey galloped towards the finish line. Gary called out our time. Carly craned her neck over his shoulder checking that the time he called corresponded with the one on the stopwatch.

'Shame,' said Carly as I pulled up. 'Two minutes behind me. How embarrassing.'

Gary frowned. 'Not to worry, Ash. You'll pick up a bit of time over the week.'

He patted Honey's sticky golden neck then hurried off.

Carly grabbed my reins.

'Get your hands off,' I spat, dropping to the ground.

Carly smiled wickedly and pushed her face close to mine, tightening her grip on my reins. 'I'd keep my eyes open if I were you, Miller. Another performance like that and I just might be able to convince Gary to *ditch* you from the team.'

'You slime!' I gasped, the full meaning of Carly's words hitting me like a runaway horse float. I knew I'd cleared that jump. 'So who was in the coat?

Ryan? Flea? It couldn't have been anyone else. It's not like you have any other friends.'

Carly laughed and threw Honey's reins at me, gliding away with Destiny as though she owned the universe.

I stood there, seething. How stupid of me! Dumb, stupid, idiot me. To fall for the oldest trick in the book. There had to be a way to catch Carly in her own trap. I just needed to figure out how to do it.

NINETEEN
The Big Event

'I can't believe I'm here, I can't believe I'm here.' I
stood on shaky legs flanked by Becky and Jenna. It
was more like they were holding me up, actually.
This was like nothing I'd ever seen. Bigger than any
gymkhana I'd ever ridden in. There were at least a
million people packed into the marshalling area at
Waratah Grove Riding Academy. Stewards in green
jackets darted here and there looking stressed. Jump
judges in blue jackets were checking maps and
looking at their watches. The smells of horses, tack,
dirt and grass were overpowering. Voices boomed
over the loudspeakers. It was chaos. I kissed Honey's
nose and rubbed at her ears, sighing aloud.

'Relax,' Becky said.

'Easy for you to say,' I said, feeling the hotel scrambled eggs I'd eaten for breakfast performing slow, cold somersaults in my stomach. Bad choice, I scolded myself, very bad indeed.

'You walked the course, didn't you?' Jenna asked, stroking Honey's firm neck.

I nodded and tugged at my chin-guard. It seemed tighter than usual. Sweat tickled the skin near my ears.

'How did it look?'

'Unggarump.'

'I think that was an "okay",' Becky said, looking at her watch. 'How did Honey's warm-up go?'

'Bffulllggem.'

'I think that was a "brilliantly"!' Jenna said, giggling.

I eyed the competition. They all looked so professional. Each was mounted on a perfectly groomed horse and dressed impeccably in their coloured zone shirts. A rider from Barrington Downs Zone gave an official a nod and gathered his reins, his grey gelding springing from the starting line on the ring of the bell.

'Look at him go,' I croaked. 'He looks like a pro.'

'Focus,' Jenna said, checking Honey's straps for the tenth time in as many minutes.

My stomach writhed with nerves. I had never felt like this before. Riding had always been so much fun, even at competitions. But there had never been so much at stake: the trophy, the money, four weeks at Waratah Grove Riding Academy. Sure they were pretty cool prizes. But weighing a little more heavily on my mind were the Creeps. How could I face them if I lost? How could I face Gary? My parents had come all this way to see me ride. I wanted them to be proud. I winced at the thought of having to tell them I'd come last. And Becky? I was taking her place. To mess up would hurt her as much as it would hurt me. And what about Honey? She trusted me. I couldn't let her down. She'd come so far. And it was up to me to make sure she went all the way to the top. After all she'd been through she deserved to be a champion. Much more than I did.

Becky's sharp, non-plastered elbow shocked me back to the moment.

'He's back,' she said, eyes on her watch. 'And about time, too.'

'Do you mean ...?' I asked hopefully.

'Way over time.' Jenna stifled a yawn.

I glanced at the rider. He shook his head in disgust, despite his perfectly clear run. He slid down from the saddle. A tall man patted the boy's back.

The second rider, in a red Acacia Falls Zone shirt, positioned herself at the starting line. I watched as her black mare tensed and burst onto the course a second before the bell rang.

'Did you see that?' Becky shrieked. 'That's cheating. You can be eliminated for that!'

I craned over Honey's neck to see the judges. A stern-faced steward beckoned to a woman also in a red shirt. They spoke loudly for a few minutes and then the woman stalked away, muttering to herself.

'Unbelievable!' Becky was wide-eyed. 'I think that girl from Acacia Falls has been eliminated!'

Jenna frowned as she strapped me into Becky's brand-new bought-for-the-Championships body protector. 'What bad luck.'

'Good luck for you though,' Becky said, nudging me again with her good elbow.

'But she was only a second or two early. Maybe it was nerves.' I bit at my bottom lip and wriggled. The body protector felt bulky and strange, a bit like a life jacket.

Becky shrugged. 'This isn't a Riding Club rally. It's the Waratah Grove Championships. The winners get to train with the best of the best.'

A jolt of electricity zapped down my spine. The best of the best? I wasn't good enough to train next to the best of the best or even behind them, much less *with* them! I wheezed, doubling over, as the next rider gathered her reins.

'Don't look now,' Jenna moaned.

Naturally, I looked.

Carly, dressed in a dark-blue T-shirt identical to mine, rode Destiny towards the starting line. She pulled the mare up, looking down at me like I was a cockroach and pointed her brand-new crop at my nose. I stared down the barrel of the crop and shuddered.

'Can't believe you're actually going through with it,' she sneered. 'If I were you I'd take that nag and bolt for the nearest cave. Which incidentally is right where you belong.'

'Nick off will ya, Carly!' Jenna spat.

'And you,' Carly went on, her cold eyes sliding

over Becky, 'get used to watching from the sidelines, Rebecca's Garden. Someone has to be Under-Twelve Champion and you're looking at her.'

'Is that so?' Becky hissed. 'Must be why I was looking right at Ashleigh.'

Carly's face went redder than her hair. She snapped the crop against Destiny's rump. The horse scrambled to a walk and took her place at the starting line beside a scowling official who was pointing to a clock. The bell rang and Carly was off.

'Nice one, Beck,' I said. 'I've never seen a human tomato before.'

'I hope Destiny's going to be okay,' Becky muttered.

The next rider went out and the next and the next. They seemed to go on forever and ever until, suddenly, Jenna pinched my arm.

'What?'

'You're up,' she squeaked. 'Now. Quick!'

'Oh, no.' My stomach rolled, letting loose at least a squillion butterflies that wasted no time in zooming around madly behind my ribs.

I pulled Honey's reins over her sweet head with trembling fingers. Becky held my stirrup and I jammed my foot inside. Clinging to the pommel I bounced up into the saddle and tried to settle in, feeling about as comfortable as I would settling onto a cactus.

The stern-faced steward approached. She grabbed Honey's reins under her chin and looked up at me.

'Ready to go?' she said.

I looked from Becky to Jenna. My best friends in the world. They smiled.

'Good luck, Ash,' Jenna said, squeezing my knee.

'Yeah, you'll knock 'em dead,' Becky added.

I swallowed and gripped my reins tightly, nodding. The words came out all by themselves.

'I'm ready.'

The bell rang. The sound seemed far away at first. Honey leaped out instinctively into a canter. For a moment I forgot what I was supposed to do, looking around at the wash of colours and noise. Under me Honey's pace increased to a gallop down the straight stretch of hoof-churned grass and mud, and in a second the first jump bore down on us. I shook my head trying to focus. It was a log, partly concealed by a low green shrub. Honey surged towards it. Too late I remembered to pull her up, to steady her for the jump. I yanked on the reins as the jump loomed. Honey shook her head, bearing down on the bit and cleared the log.

'Whoa, girl!' I yelled. 'Easy!'

Honey lowered her head, tugging the reins from my fingers and scrambled back into a mad gallop. I cursed myself. *Wake up, Ashleigh. Get with it.*

I clung to the saddle and pulled at the reins, all my lessons and training forgotten. Another jump was ahead. A fence of three white wooden rails secured to two fat brick stumps.

Honey fought me for control. Just to make sure she got her own way Honey threw her head back so far I could see the tiny stitches in her rosettes.

I braced myself as Honey soared over the jump. Thinking fast I pulled her head in and down. The bit settled in her mouth as she touched down and her wildness eased at once. I cried out, relieved, and patted her neck, my heart pumping hard behind my ribs.

I relaxed a little, looking ahead to the next jump. Honey stretched into a gallop, her hooves tearing earthy chunks from the course up into the air. I squinted into the sunlight and tried to focus. The jump came up suddenly as if from out of nowhere. It was a brush hut; a jump made from what looked like a dried-out old hedge with a tall arch over the top. I pulled Honey back into a canter and loosened her reins again, giving her her head. She tucked in her forelegs and sprang from her hind legs, soaring, then landed perfectly on the other side.

'Good girl!' I called, slapping her neck as I gathered my reins. Honey galloped on up a small hill dotted with spectators. She was growing damp with sweat. I dug my fingers into her mane, craning for a look at the next obstacle, straining my brain to remember what was coming up. I'd been so nervous and so preoccupied with Carly I'd taken in about two seconds of the course tour. Somebody screamed at us from behind the barrier and Honey lunged sideways. My stomach lurched as I grabbed at my pommel.

'Easy, girl,' I murmured, not sure if she could hear me. 'Easy.'

She calmed again and turned her attention to the course, her ears pricked forward. I could tell she was enjoying herself. It was a wild ride, galloping, soaring, darting and flying free. It was almost like she'd come home. She knew what to do. For a moment I felt like a passenger, like Honey was teaching me, showing me what to do. And both of us had something to prove, not just to the Creeps and everyone at Riding Club, but to ourselves.

Then it happened as it always did. Everything, everyone, just faded into nothingness. It was just my horse, the course and me. We sailed, we leapt. One obstacle after another, fused into one being. A water jump, a ditch, a coffin, more brush jumps and a wall just melted away underneath us. And then, suddenly, the last jump was ahead of us, a simple oxer; a fat pole balanced on two sleek stumps. Honey cleared it and landed clean. I urged her into a final gallop down the home stretch. We crossed the finish line, noise enveloping us. Then Becky and Jenna were at my feet jumping up and down and people were cheering and I could see my parents doing a Mexican wave all on their own. I fell forward onto Honey's neck.

'Thank you,' I whispered. 'You perfect horse. My Honey.'

TWENTY
Photo Finish

'You'll win for sure,' Becky said. 'You did it in just under ten minutes!'

I shook my head. 'I don't believe it. It's impossible.'

'Believe it,' Jenna said, grinning like a lunatic. 'It's the best time so far. You and Honey were amazing.'

I smiled and wrapped my arms around Honey's neck, kissing her damp coat.

'C'mon,' Becky said, loosening Honey's straps. 'Let's cool her down. She'll need to look her best for the photos!'

I laughed; relieved it was all over but a bit sad all at once. It had been so great! I was annoyed at myself for having been so nervous. I hadn't enjoyed it as much as I could have.

We walked Honey from the finish past the marshalling area and through the crowd to headquarters. I wiped at my wet forehead, suddenly conscious of the intense summer heat.

Mum rushed over and wrapped herself around me in some kind of wrestling grip.

'We're so proud!' she cried. 'You were so wonderful, Ash. Honey too.'

I gasped for air and tried to prise her fingers from around my neck. She forgets how strong she is. But that's what comes of carrying toilets around all day.

'Um, Mrs M?' Jenna said, clearing her throat. 'I think you're choking her.'

Mum released her hold on me and I sucked some delicious oxygen into my lungs.

'Thanks, Mum,' I croaked, rubbing at my throat. 'Nice biceps you've got there.'

'Ash, you were magnifico!' Dad boomed, pushing people out of the way. He planted a hairy kiss on my cheek, so excited his freckles were luminous.

'Honey was brilliant,' I said, patting her neck.

'I guess she's earned her next few meals.' Dad laughed at my shocked expression. 'Just kidding.'

Becky nudged me. 'Look.'

I peered through my crowd of well-wishers to where Carly was being comforted by her parents under a tree. She was sobbing so hard it actually sounded like 'boo hoo'. Flea and Ryan stood nearby looking uncomfortable. Gary was talking non-stop into his mobile phone, Carly's crop clenched tight in his other hand.

'Something's happened,' Jenna whispered. 'Something bad.'

'I've called you together for a moment to let you in on some news.' Gary cleared his throat and looked solemnly from one curious face to another.

I swallowed and nudged Becky in the ribs. She glanced at me and shrugged, mystified. Jenna squeezed my elbow. I turned to her and indicated Carly who was standing nearby, flanked by Flea and Ryan. Flea glared straight at me, a murderous look on his face. Ryan gazed up at the tree, his huge fists hanging at his sides like lamb roasts. I wished then and there that the fundraiser dance hadn't been such a huge success. That way Gary would never have been able to hire a bus and I wouldn't be here at Waratah Grove Riding Academy with all three Creepketeers.

'This doesn't look good,' Jenna said.

'We have had a disqualification.' Gary almost choked on the word, pale under his cap. I wondered for a second if he ever took it off.

Carly resumed her sobbing at a hundred thousand decibels. A horrible noise, like a growl, rose from Flea's throat. Ryan stared at a sparrow, pecking intently at a crust in the dust.

'Carly has been eliminated from today's competition,' Gary said as quickly as he could, almost like he could hardly bear to hear it aloud.

I gasped and turned to Becky who turned to Jenna, open-mouthed.

The three of us stared at Carly whose blotchy, tear-stained face resembled a slice of strawberry marble cake.

'It's not fair,' she howled. 'You have to do something.'

Gary shook his head. 'I've done all I can. The judges' decision is final. There are no second chances at this level. Especially not where dangerous riding is concerned!'

I shook my head. Dangerous riding! Gary had warned her. My face flushed when I thought of all the riders from the zone who could have been here instead of Carly. Riders who would rather walk the course than hurt their horses.

Carly stepped forward and pointed menacingly at Becky. 'If it was her, you'd try harder,' she shrieked. 'If it was her, you'd make sure she won first place!'

Gary's ears reddened. 'You're out of line. And you broke the rules. Your overuse of the crop equals automatic disqualification! Now you have to face the consequences of your actions.'

Carly opened her mouth, then thought better of whatever she had intended to say and snapped it shut again.

'Poor Destiny!' Becky gasped.

Gary turned on his heels and marched to the judges' table.

I turned to Becky, but before I could speak a bony finger poked at my chest.

'You set this up,' Flea barked.

I stared at him, befuddled. 'I set what up?'

'You know exactly what I'm talking about,' he snarled. 'And if you know what's good for you you'll drop out now.'

'What's that supposed to mean?' My heart began to pound.

Flea moved his face close to mine. 'Let me spell it out for ya.'

'This'll be good,' Becky sneered. 'Last spelling test you did you got minus five out of ten if I remember correctly.'

Flea curled his fist and held it close to my cheek. I felt the warmth of his skin and shivered. 'You win, Miller, and you're history in Shady Creek.'

It was all too much for Becky. She pushed Flea away, her face redder than the Acacia Falls uniforms. 'Looks like Carly's the one who's history in Shady Creek!'

Flea backed away, shaking his fist. 'Remember what I said, Miller.'

'This is it.' Becky mouthed at me from the crowd of spectators.

The last rider had completed the course and the scores had been tallied. The winner of the Waratah

Grove Junior Cross-Country Riding Championships, Under 12 Division would be announced any minute.

Each rider who had competed and not been eliminated had lined up beside the judges' table which was groaning under the weight of three golden trophies, the largest of which, the winner's cup, was big enough to bathe a baby in. On the other side of the table, three round blocks of different heights were waiting for the first, second and third place winners. I held Honey's reins under her chin with one hand and stroked her neck with the other. We'd been through so much together. And here we were at Waratah Grove. It was like a dream.

A woman, wearing a pair of green tartan knickerbockers and a matching cap grabbed a microphone, introduced herself as Mrs Annabel Strickland, the Director of the Waratah Grove Riding Academy, and began a speech. She thanked the riders, the horses, the stewards, the coaches, the parents … I tuned out.

'And now we come to the moment you've all been waiting for,' Mrs Strickland said, waking me up at last.

'The trophy for third place goes to ...' she began.

I crossed my fingers. Third place. I reckoned we had a pretty good chance for third. My maths wasn't too bad and I'd kept a vague ear on the scores as they'd been announced. Yeah, I'd be happy with third.

'Emily Warren riding Berry representing Northern Peninsula Zone!'

My heart drooped as the crowd erupted in cheers and Emily Warren, a grinning dark-haired girl leading a strawberry roan mare, accepted her trophy from Mrs Strickland and took her place on the smallest block.

The applause died down and Mrs Strickland cleared her throat. 'Second place goes to ...'

As she squinted at the sheet of paper with the winners' names on it, my pulse throbbed. Okay, so we'd missed out on third. Maybe there was a chance for second.

'Ah, second place goes to Lachlan Barlow riding Arabian Knight and representing Western Rivers Zone!'

A thoroughly stoked-looking Lachlan Barlow, dragging an exhausted grey gelding behind him, charged on Mrs Strickland, shaking her hand and grabbing his trophy. The crowd applauded. A large group of Lachlan supporters whistled and cheered. Lachlan mounted the second tallest block.

I felt terrible. It was all over. I couldn't have won. I just couldn't have. If only Becky hadn't broken her arm. If only she'd ridden instead of me.

I leant my head against Honey's while Mrs Strickland's voice announcing the winner washed over me. I hoped whoever they were that they were as happy as I was miserable.

'I'm so sorry I let you down, girl,' I said.

Honey nickered softly. I rubbed her forelock and searched the crowd for my friends. How was I going to face Becky? I had taken her place, and I had let her down.

Mrs Strickland was still talking as I found Becky and Jenna in the crowd. I expected them to look as lousy as I felt. They didn't. I frowned, curious as my crazy best friends jumped up and down, hugging each other. Surely they weren't happy I'd lost? What kind of friends were they anyway?

'Excuse me,' said a voice on my right. I peered around a huge bay mare.

'Yes?'

'Are you Ashleigh Miller?' The mare's rider, a rosy-cheeked girl in a lavender Coastal Zone T-shirt, regarded me.

I nodded.

She raised her eyebrows. 'You're being called.'

Mrs Strickland's voice boomed out of the enormous speakers.

'Would Ashleigh Miller, riding Honey and representing Shady Creek and Districts Zone, please come forward to accept first place. This trophy is getting rather heavy!'

I pounded on my ear with my fist. Surely there was a potato growing in it. It sounded like I was being called to accept the trophy. That couldn't be right.

I looked back at Jenna and Becky who were screaming at me to move my butt. I saw Gary waving his cap at me, and what looked suspiciously like tears creeping down his dusty face. It was true!

I tugged gently on Honey's reins and took a step forward. The judges' table seemed to be an age away. Each step lasted a lifetime. The crowd roared in my ears. A chant — *Ashleigh, Ashleigh, Ashleigh* —

echoed around the stadium. Mrs Strickland beamed at me as Honey and I approached.

'Congratulations, Miss,' she said, pumping my hand vigorously and thrusting a cheque into the other. Next she heaved the trophy into my arms. Holding onto the handles, I stared at it, dumbstruck. Engraved in beautiful flowing letters was an inscription — *Waratah Grove Junior Cross-Country Riding Under-12 Champions: Ashleigh Miller and Honey*.

'Th-thanks,' I stammered. 'Thanks a lot.'

I led Honey to the middle block, the tallest one, and climbed up, barely able to hold on to our trophy, the cheque and Honey's reins. The crowd cheered louder than ever. I saw them all: my friends Jenna and Becky, Jodie and Julie; Gary, and Mum and Dad who were hugging each other and madly snapping photo after photo.

I planted a big kiss on Honey's head just as Mrs Strickland fastened the blue ribbon I'd dreamed of around her sweet neck. We had done it.

TWENTY-ONE

Horse Mad Summer

'I can't believe it's my last night here in Shady Creek.' Jenna poked a stick into our campfire and leant back on her heels, her arms wrapped around her bare legs.

We had swum in the pool for hours and eaten an end-of-summer-holidays feast of hot dogs with lashings of rich red tomato sauce.

'Anyone want to toast marshmallows?' Becky asked, threading one fat white marshmallow after another onto a reasonably straight twig. 'I brought two whole bags just in case.'

'Nah, I always burn them,' I said, staring into the red and orange flames. 'So unless you do the cooking I'll have mine raw. By the way, thanks for bringing your tent around. It's perfect.'

The three of us twisted around and admired the Chos' tent, which we'd pitched in the yard beside Honey's paddock.

'S'okay,' Becky said, scratching under her cast. 'Dad bought it during his outback survival phase and it's never seen the light of day. That's what Mum says anyway.'

'What are you gonna do with your thousand bucks?' Jenna asked, reaching into the bag of marshmallows.

I shrugged. 'Spend it all on Honey I s'pose. And long-distance phone calls.'

Silence fell over us for a while, each of us lost in our own thoughts as Becky toasted marshmallows and we popped them, sticky and warm, into our mouths. I thought about the last month and about how after tomorrow, Honey and I would wake up alone: Jenna back home in the city, Cassata back home at Becky's. My heart squeezed. I would miss them both so much. But Jenna especially. When she'd first arrived it had seemed like she'd be in

Shady Creek forever and now our time together was already over.

When we were full we lay back on the grass, warming our toes with the fire and staring up at the night sky, which glittered with more stars than I had ever seen in the city. Insects chirruped and the horses tore at the grass nearby, munching on a late-night snack.

'So how are you gonna cope back home?' Becky said suddenly. 'You know, with your parents.'

Jenna rolled over onto her stomach and picked at the grass. 'Dunno. I'm not sure I want to go back home. Everything'll be packed up and in boxes. They've sold the house. Mum called and told me a few days ago.'

I sat up, gasping. 'Why didn't you say so?'

Jenna shrugged. 'You had the Championships to worry about. And I needed some time to think.'

'That's awful,' Becky said quietly. 'It's so awful.'

'Don't worry,' Jenna said as casually as she could although I knew her heart was breaking.

'Where are you going to live?' I said. I couldn't believe it. Jenna had always lived on my old street. All these changes! My head spun as I tried to take it all in.

'At Grandma's. Just for a bit while we find a new place. Dad's already got a unit though, right near school. He said it's got a bedroom for me for when I stay over. We're gonna go shopping and get all new things.'

'You sound so calm,' Becky said thoughtfully. 'If it was me I'd be freaking out!'

'I've been thinking a lot while I've been here. Trail rides are good for thinking, that's one thing I've learned about horses!' Jenna frowned. 'I'm starting to understand now — it's not that they don't love me any more, or my brat brothers. They just don't love each other. They'll be happier apart.'

'Wow,' I said. Jenna sounded so grown-up. 'Will you be happy?'

'I've been thinking about that, too. When Mum and Dad first told us they were getting divorced all I wanted was for them to stay together. I would have given anything ...' Jenna gazed up at the sky for a moment, then smiled at Becky and me, her braces twinkling in the firelight. 'But I'm going to be okay. We all are. It's just going to be different. Look, thanks for putting up with me. And for listening. You're a real friend, Ash.'

I grinned. 'You can always come and live here with me.'

'Anytime,' Becky said.

'Thanks, but I reckon Mum'd get a bit lonely with only the terrible two for company.'

'So will Becky and I,' I said. 'What are we s'posed to do now that it's three against two again?'

Jenna grinned. 'You can handle the Creeps.'

'Jenna, I think all this fresh country air has gotten to your head. Have you forgotten what Flea said to me at Waratah Grove? The Creepketeers are going to make our lives a misery once we're back at school.'

Jenna smiled. 'You know they're the one thing I won't miss about Shady Creek.'

'How about taking them home with you?' Becky said. 'I don't think anyone will mind!'

We collapsed in giggles. It was unreal.

We put out the fire and crawled into the tent, nestling into our sleeping bags. It wasn't long before Becky and Jenna fell asleep, their breathing deep and rhythmic. I lay awake between my two best friends wishing like nothing I'd ever wished for that things would never ever change.

I stood alone in my room staring at the space where Jenna's bed had been. She'd been gone for only a few hours and already I missed her so much it was like a deep throbbing pain in my chest.

'How does it feel to have your room all to yourself again, possum?'

I spun around. Mum and Dad had poked their heads through the door and were watching me intently.

'I miss Jenna,' I said, turning my gaze to all the places in my room that reminded me Jenna had gone. The empty drawers, the half-empty wardrobe, my old helmet and joddies placed neatly on the end of my bed. 'I hate it when things change. Why can't everything stay the same?'

Mum took a step inside my room and leant on the doorway. 'We'd never have come to Shady Creek.'

'You'd never have rescued Honey,' Dad added.

'Jenna would never have come to stay in the first place.'

'You'd never have gone to the Championships.'

I threw up my hands in despair. 'Okay, okay. I think I get it. But that doesn't stop me missing her.'

I sat on my bed. Mum sat beside me and squeezed my knee. Dad stayed put in the doorway, a strange smile spread across his face. He looked like the cat that had got not only the cream, but the budgie as well.

'Looking forward to the camp?' Mum asked.

I shivered. 'Waratah Grove Riding Academy. I can't believe I'm actually going.'

'Believe it, kid,' Dad said. 'Your mum and I can't wait.'

I frowned. 'What do you mean?'

'It'll be like a second honeymoon for us!'

'Yuck!' I made a face and threw my pillow at him.

Mum patted my leg. 'Ash, we have some news.'

'You're coming with me?'

She shook her head.

'Flea's place is up for sale?'

Another shake.

My heart dropped into my stomach. 'Don't tell me. You're splitting up, aren't you? Like the Dawsons!'

'Quite the opposite,' Dad said, that same strange smile spreading from ear to ear. 'Congratulations are in order, Ashleigh Louise. Your mum's pregnant!'

My mouth dropped open. I stared from one of them to the other hardly able to believe what I'd just heard. A baby! At their age!

'Well?' Mum said, a hopeful smile playing around her lips.

'It's great news!' I jumped up then pulled Mum to her feet and wrapped my arms around her neck.

'Really?' she said. 'Are you pleased?'

I was. Jenna coming to stay had given me a real taste for having a sister. I knew Becky would tell me I was insane but I wanted this baby. 'Yes. Definitely yes. I hope it's a girl!'

'Who knows?' Dad mused as he walked towards us. He slipped his arm around Mum's waist. 'Maybe it'll be a boy.'

'If it's a girl can we call her Jenna?'

Mum raised her eyebrows. 'We'll see.'

'Or Rebecca? How about Rebecca?'

'Ashleigh, relax! We have months to decide.'

'How many months? When will the baby be

here?' I stepped back and examined my mother. 'You don't look pregnant.'

Mum smiled. 'It's incredible what work overalls can disguise. Anyway, we'll tell you everything over dinner.'

'Which we'd better get started on,' Dad said, looking at his watch.

'Good, I'm starved,' I said. I waved them out my room. 'Now if you'll excuse me I have some work to do.'

Mum looked confused. 'Like what? You don't go back to school until next week.'

I sighed. Sometimes I just don't get grown-ups. 'I have to baby-proof my room. I don't want the kid getting their hands on my headless horse clock.'

'It's a timeless piece of equine art, right?' Dad said, grinning. He held out his arms and I fell gratefully into a warm cuddle. Mum wrapped her arms around the both of us.

'Right.'

Waratah Grove, a thousand dollrs to spend, a baby, the Creeps ... somehow I knew my adventures in Shady Creek were only just beginning.

Acknowledgements

I would like to thank my publisher at HarperCollins, Lisa Berryman, and my editor Lydia Papandrea for their guidance and support. Thank you also to my husband and horsy-destination finder, Bill, the totally horse mad Nina Burnett and Evangeline Read, my always encouraging family and friends and Clarrie — thank you for the horse mad summers.

The Publisher and Author would like to thank all those involved with the cover: Photographer, Belinda Taylor (www.bellaphotoart.com.au); Models, Gabriella Power (Ashleigh, front and back cover) and Annika Blau (Jenna, back cover); Cash and Cash's owner, Grahame Ware Jr (www.livestockforfilms.com.au); and Horseland Artarmon, NSW (www.horseland.com.au) who supplied the clothing.

Photo by Dyan Hallworth

KATHY HELIDONIOTIS grew up in Sydney living for the school holidays, which she spent on the New South Wales south coast studying the three essential 'Rs': reading, writing and riding (horses, of course). She now divides her time between writing stories, reading good books, teaching and looking after her three gorgeous children. Kathy has had nine children's books published so far. *Horse Mad Summer* follows the popular *Totally Horse Mad*.

Visit Kathy at her website:

www.kathyhelidoniotis.com

Kathy Helidoniotis

HORSE MAD
1

totally
Horse
MAD

It's all about friendship,
fun and a passion
for horses

Totally Horse Mad

I had a great idea. Maybe I could buy Princess. Then she'd really be mine, not just a horse I rode once a week … I made up my mind. If it was the last thing I did, I was going to get my very own horse.

The only things that stand between Ashleigh Miller and the horse of her dreams are a whole lot of dollars that she doesn't have, parents who don't know one end of a horse from another and a city backyard the size of a shoebox.

Ashleigh can't believe it when her parents announce that she will finally have a horse of her own, but at a price she could never have imagined. She will have to say goodbye to her best friend, Jenna, South Beach Stables and her favourite horse, Princess. Ashleigh and her family are leaving the city and heading for Shady Creek, a small country town. And that's where the adventures in this Horse Mad series really begin.

Coming soon, the third book in this exciting series
for the horse crazy at heart!

Horse Mad Academy

BOOK 3 AVAILABLE FROM
DECEMBER 2006

*I spun around slowly on the spot, taking everything in. I
couldn't believe it. A year ago I was living in the city in a small
house, with an even smaller backyard, riding once a week and
dreaming that one day I would have a horse of my own. Now
Honey and I were at Waratah Grove – one of the best riding
academies in the country! The next four weeks are going to be
like one long beautiful Horse Mad dream. I know I'm going to
love it here!*

The Junior Cross-Country Riding Championships are
over and Ashleigh Miller has arrived at Waratah Grove
Riding Academy. It's a dream come true for any Horse
Mad kid, but as Ashleigh discovers, things don't always
turn out like you hope they will. With a gruelling riding
schedule, training with the best junior riders in Australia, a
horse who just refuses to do dressage and a chance to ride
at the Nationals up for grabs, Ashleigh is starting to think
that life in Shady Creek with the Creepketeers is simple.

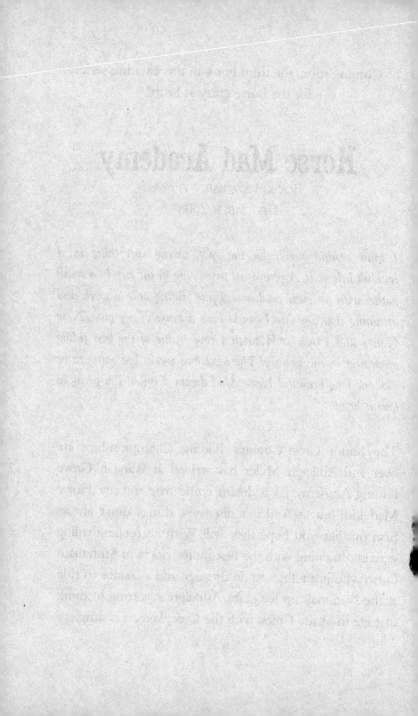